ESPECIALLY FOR GIRLS ™
presents

CONFESSIONS OF A PRIME TIME KID

MARK JONATHAN HARRIS

LOTHROP, LEE & SHEPARD BOOKS
NEW YORK

FOR MY MOTHER

This book is a presentation of
Especially for Girls™
Weekly Reader Books.

Weekly Reader Books offers book clubs for children from
preschool through high school.

For further information write to:
Weekly Reader Books
4343 Equity Drive
Columbus, Ohio 43228

Especially for Girls™
is a trademark of Weekly Reader Books.

Grateful acknowledgment is made to the following for permission to reprint copyrighted material:

CBS Robbins Catalog Inc. for the lyrics from "Singin' in the Rain" on page 31. Words by Arthur Freed, music by Nacio Herb Brown © 1929, renewed 1957 by Metro-Golden-Mayer Inc. Rights assigned to CBS Catalogue Partnership. All rights controlled and administered by CBS Robbins Catalog Inc. All rights reserved. International copyright secured. Used by permission.

Harper & Row Publishers, Inc. for the last five stanzas of "Why Nobody Pets the Lion at the Zoo" on page 116, from *The Reason for the Pelican* by John Ciardi (J.B. Lippincott Company). Copyright © 1959 by John Ciardi. Reprinted by permission of Harper & Row Publishers, Inc.

Library of Congress Cataloging in Publication Data

Harris, Mark Jonathan, (date)
    Confessions of a prime time kid.

    Summary: A thirteen-year-old television star writes her memoirs, explaining the difficulties and joys of her unusual life.
    1. Children's stories, American. [1. Actors and actresses—Fiction.
2. Television—Fiction. 3. Single-parent family—Fiction] I. Title.
PZ7.H24229Co   1985   [Fic] 84-20144
ISBN 0-688-03979-0

CONTENTS

Margaret O'Brien Muldaur Raps *with* Super Teen

All Meg Muldaur has to do is look at you, smile, and you melt . . . right? Well, you'd better believe it, for this *Kid and the Cabbie* star has all the girlish charm needed to literally sweep you off your feet. She knows she's lucky, she knows it's terrific to be a big TV star . . . but Meg hasn't let any of it go to her head. We caught up with her recently for a few questions.

ST: Did you always want to be an actress?
MEG: I don't know about always, but I've been acting ever since I was six. I don't remember what I wanted to do before that.
ST: If you weren't an actress, what would you want to be?
MEG: I don't know. I haven't thought much about that . . . . maybe a checker at the grocery store. Yeah, I think I'd like that. You'd get to meet a lot of people.
ST: What do you think of your fans?
MEG: Well, I'm flattered by all the mail they send me, but I don't understand it. If they knew me, I think they'd find me real dull. It makes me sad that they take all that

time to write me. The truth is I don't have time to answer their letters. A secretary does it for me.

ST: What do you like to do in your spare time?

MEG: I don't have much spare time, but one thing I like to do after work is stand in the shower and pretend to be Gene Kelly dancing in *Singin' in the Rain*. I'm developing a pretty fair Gene Kelly routine.

ST: What do you like to spend your money on?

MEG: Tapes and records and chocolate truffles. L.A. has some terrific candy stores and I've tried out the truffles at a lot of them. I love white chocolate, too.

ST: How about clothes?

MEG: I like jeans and T-shirts. That's what I wear most. I have a great collection of T-shirts, but my mom prefers I wear dresses, so she picks them out.

ST: Who are your fave actors?

MEG: Well, like my mom, I love anybody who can really dance— Gene Kelly, Fred Astaire, John Travolta. But I guess my real favorites are actors like Wallace Snyder, or Dustin Hoffman, who can play practically any part. I loved Dustin Hoffman in *Tootsie*.

ST: How about actresses?

MEG: Judy Garland in *The Wizard of Oz*, Debbie Reynolds when she was young, Tatum O'Neal before she grew up. I like lots of people. Goldie Hawn, Meryl Streep, anybody, really, who can make me laugh or cry.

ST: What's your pet peeve?

MEG: People who talk about the ratings all the time . . . or box office grosses, or the stock market.

ST: What do you like to do on dates?

MEG: I don't know. I've never been on a date.

ST: Well, what kind of men attract you?

MEG: Older men, you know, like around forty.

She smiled when she said that, boys, a smile that would melt your heart, but that's Meg Muldaur for you, a star without a swelled head who still enjoys being a kid. This year she turns thirteen. All you older men, watch out!

SAWDUST MEMORIES

When the story came out that I had run away from home, I received more mail than I did for any show I had ever done. Some of the people called me spoiled and ungrateful and said they'd never liked me on television anyway. Others said they couldn't understand why I'd ever want to run away. "You seemed like such a happy child," one woman from Atlanta, Georgia, wrote.

Reading through the hundreds of letters I received, I realized how little people really knew me. They thought I was the same person they saw every week on *The Kid and the Cabbie* or the "impish little girl" they read about in *TV Guide*. But what they saw on TV or read about in the fan magazines is only part of what I'm like—a very small part, really—and I wanted a chance to tell the rest without a press expert from the network interrupting.

When my agent, Rhonda Cohen, heard that I was thinking of writing the story of my life, she immediately telephoned and told me to stop. "Writing your memoirs at thirteen is in *extremely* bad taste," she warned. "If an actress is going to be rude enough to write her autobiography, she should at least have the good grace to wait until she's in her sixties and all the people she's gossiping about are dead. When you're too old to get any more good parts, then you can tell all. For now it's better to keep it to yourself."

I've thought a lot about Rhonda's advice, but I don't agree. Even though I may seem a little young to be telling my life story, a lot has happened to me. My brother Kelly, who started acting as a kid, too, also thinks it's a good idea to write this. "Somebody's got to tell the truth about what it's like for kid actors," he says. "Don't chicken out, Meg, and don't try to make any of us look good. Just tell it like it is."

So I have. Some people, including Kelly, might not like everything I say here (or me either, I guess), but at least it's the truth.

Since my mom named my brother and me after two of her favorite film stars, perhaps it's not surprising that we both ended up in show business. But then Darlene—that's my mom—has always been "movie-crazy," as my grandma says. The week before Kelly was born, Grandma told us the theater down the street was running a festival of old Gene Kelly musicals; and the night before Mom went to the hospital to have me she saw Margaret O'Brien in *Little Women* at the same theater. Kelly and I have often wondered what she would have called us if the theater had been showing a festival of Bela Lugosi horror films or an Elvis Presley series.

Darlene told me she responded to our births the way she does to all her favorite movies: she cried. When Kelly was born she didn't stop for almost two weeks afterward; when I came along fourteen months later she only cried for about a week. I'm not sure, however, if that was a sign of any great improvement on her part. She claims she cried over Kelly because he was so beautiful and over me because she had always wanted a daughter. In fact, I have my doubts that I was exactly what she had in mind. You see, I've seen my baby pictures, and if you want to know the truth, I was pretty ugly, all puckered and misshapen—a face, as they say, that only a mother could love. I think mine may definitely have had reservations.

I suppose Darlene had other reasons for tears, though. As she'll be the first to admit, she wasn't really ready for motherhood. Kelly was born six months after Mom and Dad were married. He was eight pounds, three ounces, and in the hospital photograph taken the day after his birth he doesn't look the least premature.

Darlene says she was so delighted with Kelly, though, that she decided to have a daughter, and pretty soon there I was. Despite her tearful welcome, Darlene says that she's never had any regrets, that being a mother is the most satisfying thing she's ever done in her life. What Dad thought, I have no idea. Although there are no reports of his crying in the delivery room, he clearly had second thoughts about his family, for two months before my fifth birthday, he suddenly packed his bags and set off for Oregon without us.

I don't have many memories of my father, so it's hard to tell you what he was like then. The few things I do recall of him are a little blurry, the way dreams are when you try to remember them the next morning. I do remember Kelly and I flying kites with him on the beach, though. There was one particular day, just after my fourth birthday, that stands out pretty clearly. Dad had given me a beautiful, hand-painted eagle kite for a present, and he took Kelly and me out to test it. I wanted to fly it all by myself, of course, but it was a windy day and the kite was difficult to handle, so Dad picked me up in his arms and helped me guide it. Kelly kept tugging at Dad's arm to put me down and give him a chance. Finally he got so mad waiting for his turn that he kicked Dad in the shins. That definitely got his attention. He set me down and tore after Kelly. Unfortunately, without his help, I lost control of the kite and it nose-dived into the ocean like a wounded bird. When we pulled it out of the water the fragile paper wings were torn and mangled. I'm sure I moped for days. It's funny, though, I've talked to Kelly about that day several times, and he doesn't remember it at all.

Another early memory I have of Dad is the smell of sawdust. When he and Mom got married, he was a carpenter's apprentice in L.A. I remember picking wood shavings out of his sandy hair as he lifted me to kiss him, and the feel of his stubbly beard upon my cheek. But to be honest, after he ran out on us, I did not think about him that much.

The clearest image I have of my dad from those early years is not a memory but a color snapshot, one of the few photographs Darlene kept of the four of us together. It was taken at the beach about a year before Dad decided to split. We were all in bathing suits. Dad had one arm around Mom and the other tightly around my shoulder. (My red hair was frizzy as usual but my freckles didn't show up on the print.) Kelly was standing in front of Darlene and she had her hand on his head as if to hold him in place. Dad was muscular and handsome and Darlene was as pretty as a bathing suit model. In the photograph we looked like a perfect family, the kind you see on travel posters, having a wonderful time in Hawaii or Miami Beach. I used to look at that photograph and wonder what went wrong.

Darlene rarely talked about it. When Ryan—that's what we've called Dad ever since the spring he left—walked out on us, it was as if he ceased to exist. Only the occasional birthday cards he sent (always with a ten or twenty inside) reminded us that he was still our father.

Darlene may have bawled for weeks over Kelly's and my birth, but neither of us remember her shedding any tears over Ryan's hasty departure. I knew, though, that Dad would never return when I saw Darlene on the terrace of our apartment methodically ripping the shirts and underwear that he had left behind. One by one she dropped them on the charcoal grill and watched them burn. Some things you never forget.

FROM ORICK TO CULVER CITY

When Darlene ran off to Hollywood at seventeen, I'm sure she never dreamed that eight years later she'd wake up one morning with no husband, no job, and two little kids to feed. It was not exactly what she had in mind when she bought a one-way bus ticket from Orick to L.A.

Orick, where she grew up, is a small, fairy-talelike town on the coast of northern California surrounded by fog and mist and giant redwood trees. Grandma lives in an old two-story house on the top of a hill; when the fog rolls out in the afternoon you can see the ocean from her kitchen window. When I first visited there, it looked like Oz to me. At that time Darlene, Kelly, and I lived in a cramped two-bedroom apartment in L.A.; our kitchen looked out over the parking lot of the next-door apartment. But as beautiful as Orick is, Darlene couldn't wait until she was old enough to leave it.

Neither Grandma nor Mom have ever said much about the trouble Darlene got into as a teenager, but when Grandma called to wish me a happy twelfth birthday she said, "When your mom was your age she discovered two things, boys and movies. After that there was no talking to her. It's too late to keep you from the movies, but I hope you wait a few years to take up with boys."

Although Darlene rarely mentions her Orick boyfriends, she talks about movies all the time. There was only one movie theater in Orick, but everyone had a television set, and it was on TV that she discovered Hollywood musicals. She says one reason she fell in love with them was because they reminded her of her father, who used to sing show tunes to her when he tucked her in bed at night, and who died when she was ten. The other reason was the movies themselves. If you've ever seen them, you'll know why. When they're over you always feel like dancing in the streets yourself.

Darlene has told me how every weekend she and her girlfriends would stay up late watching *Hollywood Showcase* and imagining themselves waltzing through life in the arms of Fred Astaire or Gene Kelly. Grandma thought they were a little crazy. "Your grandma used to complain all the time," Darlene said to me once, imitating Grandma when she is giving one of her sermons about life. "'Life is not a Hollywood musical. Watching those old movies will just give you a warped view of the world.' And maybe she was right. Still, if the choice was between living like Fred Astaire and Ginger Rogers, or spending the rest of my life in Orick, there was no question what I wanted."

As soon as she graduated from high school, Darlene packed her bags and headed for L.A., determined never to return home. And she didn't until her stepfather was killed in a logging accident. That was when I first saw Orick. Up till then, Grandma kept in touch with letters and phone calls—she even came to visit a few times and sent some money after Ryan left—but basically Darlene was on her own.

Hollywood turned out to be a lot different than she had expected. Although I think Darlene's a knockout—she looks a little like a blond Natalie Wood—there are a lot of beautiful women who want to be in show business. Darlene had never acted and had no other training. In fact, the only job she'd ever had was scooping ice cream at Baskin-Robbins in Orick, which was one of the places she ended up working in L.A., too. The only job she could find in the movie business was selling popcorn and candy at Grauman's Chinese Theater, but the pay, she used to joke, was peanuts. After waitressing and modeling, she found steady work as a cocktail waitress in a nightclub. In the two years after she left home, the only person who discovered her was Ryan.

Darlene and Ryan moved into an apartment in Culver City, an older, run-down section of Los Angeles. Their apartment was just half a mile from the MGM Studios, where all the forties and fifties musicals that Darlene loved were made. But that was the closest her life came to them. Dad didn't turn out to be Fred Astaire any more than she turned out to be Ginger Rogers. In the end, though, it wasn't Darlene, but Ryan, who called it quits.

A few weeks after Ryan left us Darlene got a job selling cosmetics at Bullock's, a fancy department store in Westwood (a neighborhood on the west side of L.A. where there are a lot of movie theaters and expensive shops). Darlene didn't like the work much, but she didn't know what else to do. And that's where she was when Hollywood Dance entered our lives.

HEEL AND TOE,
FLEX AND POINT

Darlene was determined that we were not going to make the same mistakes that she did: We were going to be better prepared for life. So shortly after she started working at Bullock's, she enrolled Kelly in a tap and ballet class for first-graders. She said that whether Kelly went into show business or not, the lessons were important—they'd teach him grace and poise, for instance. Kelly thought soccer or baseball might teach him more useful skills, but without Ryan around to push for sports, Darlene got her way.

Actually, Kelly didn't argue much. Darlene had already introduced us to Gene Kelly in the late-night movies we watched on our old color TV (a wedding present from Ryan to Darlene). Both of us were impressed. If dance classes could teach you to move like that, we thought, maybe they would be fun. Unfortunately, Darlene said, she could only afford lessons for one of us. Since Kelly was older, he was chosen.

Even so, I got to tag along on Saturday mornings when Darlene drove Kelly to his weekly lessons. I don't know how Darlene had heard of the Hollywood Dance Studios—maybe she had picked it out of the Yellow Pages—but it was located in a pretty scuzzy neighborhood. Culver City wasn't anywhere near as ritzy as

Westwood, with its gleaming glass apartment buildings and its Spanish houses surrounded by neat lawns and flower gardens, but it was classy next to crummy Hollywood. I remember staring at the bums sleeping in the doorways. At first they made me nervous but after a while you got used to stepping around or over them as you climbed the stairs to the second floor studios. I don't know what kind of offices were on the first floor of that run-down building. Whoever worked there, though, must have worn ear plugs, for you could hear the clicks and shuffles of the tap shoes halfway up the street.

Inside, the walls were lined with photographs of stars who had either taken lessons there or were friends of Sonny Raskin, the owner of the school. I remember looking at those pictures many times, searching for Gene Kelly or Debbie Reynolds, or *anybody* I knew from television. But I recognized more faces in the photographs in our neighborhood deli than in those hanging in the studio. Darlene said that Sonny had been a famous dancer himself in Hollywood musicals of the forties. I think she may have been stretching the truth, though, for I've yet to see a movie in which I spotted him.

By the time Kelly started taking lessons, Sonny was pretty old. Looking more like a bald, fidgety beanpole than a movie star, he pranced around the mirrored rooms in jazz pants with a Hollywood Dance Studios T-shirt in the summer and a Hollywood Dance Studios sweatshirt in the winter. No matter what the season, though, he always looked grumpy. He didn't teach group lessons, only private ones. Everyone, however, was encouraged to buy his records. On these he personally spoke the instructions set to music: "Heel and toe, flex and point; squeeze the left knee and down, squeeze the right knee and down. Squeeze both knees and down. Open your arms and see the sky." Unfortunately, when you opened your arms and looked upward at the Hollywood Dance Studios, all you saw was crumbling plaster.

I didn't care about the cracks in the ceiling, of course, or the drunks sleeping on the staircase. I loved Hollywood Dance, the worn and ripply wooden floor, the smell of sweat, the pink palm trees painted on the wall between the huge mirrors that somehow seemed to make everything look larger. Even though I was not enrolled I remember bounding up the stairs every Saturday filled with excitement. If only I could have lessons, then maybe I, too, could glide through the world as effortlessly, as magically, as my brother's namesake.

The instructor who taught Kelly's group was a bouncy young woman named Jennifer, who never appeared to tire of going through the same steps week after week. "Right, tap, tap, together, change. Left tap, tap . . ."

"The left foot, not the right one, Mary. Do you know which one is left? That's it."

We bought the first Sonny Raskin album and I memorized it at home along with Kelly. Since Darlene couldn't afford lessons for me, she didn't buy me black patent leather tap shoes either, so I made my own taps by sticking thumb tacks to the bottoms of my sneakers. They clacked rather than tapped, but they were better than plain rubber soles. I only wore them around the house, though, never when we went for Kelly's lessons. Jennifer got so used to seeing me at the studio that she finally let me do all the steps by myself, off to the side. Then Darlene bought me some tights and a leotard, so I almost looked like everyone else. A few times Jennifer even came over and corrected me. It wasn't the same as taking lessons, but I was happy to be noticed.

Kelly was definitely the most talented of his group. When Jennifer handed out the gold stars at the end of each lesson, he always got more than anyone else. And he deserved them. It wasn't just that he knew his right foot from his left, or could do a better kick or shuffle step, but he moved in a way the other kids didn't. Although I couldn't explain it at the time, I think I sensed he had more of what it takes to be a dancer.

Sonny Raskin must have thought so, too, for one day he took

Darlene aside and encouraged her to enroll Kelly for more lessons. I don't know how many times since I've heard her repeat his advice. "Your son has promise," he lectured her, "but so do hundreds of kids who pass through here. The difference between promise and progress is discipline." Darlene didn't need convincing. "When I was a kid I didn't have any sense of discipline," she frequently reminded us. "I didn't take school or anything very seriously, and look at where I ended up. I'm not going to let the same thing happen to you."

The only problem was that discipline didn't come cheaply. Private lessons were much more expensive than a group. Darlene would have to stand behind the cosmetics counter a lot longer to earn that money than it would take Kelly to dance it away. When I overheard her talking to Sonny Raskin about extended payments, I knew it might be a long time before I got real tap shoes.

I didn't mind, though, because if Kelly didn't deserve private lessons, I didn't know who did. Not only was he handsome—with Darlene's finely chiseled features and Ryan's ruddy coloring—but he also had the talent, what Darlene jokingly called "Fred Astaire feet." I have a snapshot that Darlene took of the two of us that winter, just before Kelly started taking lessons with Sonny. It captures us perfectly at that time: we are both in tights and leotards; Kelly, in ballet slippers, is poised in first position, confident as usual; slipperless, I am standing in the same position, with my feet slightly awry. Kelly looks as if he could have been a model for a Danskin ad; I look like a pudgy kid you'd pick to sell peanut butter. If someone had asked me what I wanted most then, I'm sure I would have said "to be like my brother."

Besides, he was my closest friend, the one I spent the most time with. We shared a room and we shared Darlene. The first year after Ryan left, Darlene didn't go out much, and when she wasn't working at Bullock's, she was usually with us. One of our favorite pastimes was to dress up in costumes and stage our own shows. I'd put on Darlene's jewelry and makeup and wear one of her blouses as a dress. Kelly would don an old top hat, a Darlene thrift shop find, and twirl a cane he made from a stick. Darlene managed to look even more beautiful draped in scarves or transformed by some of the wild rummage sale castoffs she collected. Then the three of us would perform for imaginary audiences.

Sometimes Kelly and I made up our own plays. In one we were "Super Kids," survivors of the same planet as Superman, and with the same superpowers. Like Clark Kent, we'd duck into a closet, rip off our regular clothes, and emerge in blue ski pajamas with red *S*'s pinned to our chests and red towels for capes. Then we'd rescue Darlene from whatever evil she was facing. "Wait a minute. This is a job for Super Kids." Sometimes the perils we saved her from were real, like a sink full of dirty dishes, but more often they were make-believe, like fiery dragons or wicked princes.

Our most polished performances, though, were saved for scenes from our favorite movie musicals—*The Sound of Music, The Wizard of Oz, Singin' in the Rain.* Julie Andrews, Judy Garland, and Gene Kelly would probably have doubled over in laughter to see us take their parts, but what we lacked in technique we made up for in enthusiasm. The entire apartment was our sound stage, the furniture our set. Darlene let us tap dance on the kitchen table, leap from sofa to armchair, do somersaults on her bed. Afterward she'd make lemonade and popcorn. Then we'd all snuggle up in her double bed and watch TV until we finally fell asleep among the kernel-littered sheets.

Occasional treats came on Saturdays. In the morning we'd pile into "the Disgrace," the dented Honda Darlene couldn't afford to fix, and drive to Hollywood for Kelly's dancing lessons. For lunch, Darlene might take us out somewhere, like Schwab's (the famous Hollywood drugstore where Lana Turner was discovered) for hamburgers or for ice-cream sodas. Sometimes the excuse was a holiday, like Valentine's Day, but sometimes it would just be a splurge. "Go on, order whatever you want," Darlene would say when we looked over the menu. "You can't live your whole life on peanut butter and jelly." Darlene seemed to look forward to these Saturday flings as much as we did. "I don't know what I'd do without you guys," she'd say. "You're absolutely the best friends I've got."

That year I think we probably were Darlene's best, and only, friends. Sometimes, at night, I'd hear her talking on the phone to one of the women from Bullock's, but she rarely saw those ladies outside of work. She also gradually stopped seeing many of the friends that she and Ryan had had. If she missed them at all, or Ryan, she didn't say, and we never asked. It was no accident that *Singin' in the Rain* was our favorite musical.

> "Let the stormy clouds chase
>   everyone from the place.
> Come on with the rain,
> I've a smile on my face."

DANCING LIKE A BEE

Every April, Sonny Raskin rented a high school auditorium for his students' annual recital. Even though the school was hardly Hollywood's finest, casting directors and talent agents usually attended Sonny's shows. In L.A., some talent agents would even go to Sunday school plays looking for kids who might have a future in the business.

By recital time I was officially taking Saturday lessons at Hollywood Dance, too. Once Kelly began his half-hour private class, Sonny agreed to give Darlene a break on my group lessons. For class, Jennifer found me hand-me-down tap shoes and ballet slippers that some of her students had outgrown. For the recital, though, Sonny had costumes specially made, and in order to be in the show you had to pay an extra costume fee. Unfortunately, Darlene could only afford the fee for one of us. Being the more talented, Kelly naturally was the one.

Even so, I was crushed. "Next year, I promise you, it will be different," Darlene vowed. I remember tears glistening in her eyes, but those tears may have really been my own. "I understand," I mumbled before running off to my room to cry into my pillow.

I knew, though, that Darlene couldn't afford two sets of costumes. As it was, in addition to her job at Bullock's, she was now working two nights a week as a cocktail waitress to support us. Still, I was broken-hearted. Sometimes I thought if only Ryan were still living with us, we wouldn't have to worry about things like costume fees or ice-cream sodas on Saturdays.

My tears couldn't bring Ryan back, however, or earn any more money to make our lives easier. I wasn't sure exactly what could change our luck, but listening to the mothers talk around the dance studio, it sounded as if the recital might be it. At last year's show, for example, a casting director had simply fallen in love with that cute Benjy Carter and hired him on the spot for a dog food commercial. Six-year-old Benjy was now making more money than his father, the mothers said. Having become so rich and famous, Benjy had left Hollywood Dance behind, but there were other students still there who had agents and made the rounds of casting calls. From the questions Darlene asked, I could tell she was interested. If some of the other kids could get commercial work, why couldn't Kelly? After all, didn't everyone agree that he had promise?

For his part, Kelly seemed to practice for the recital all the time. He had a feature solo in one of the biggest tap numbers and a smaller role in another. In his solo he wore a top hat and tails and a fancy white satin shirt. He got to do buck-and-wings and even tricks like the "coffee grinder," where you spin around on one leg, and "falling off a log," which looks a little like it sounds. He rehearsed his solo so much that before long I knew all the steps to it, too. When I tried to practice it with him, though—as we'd done for months of class drills—he got angry. It was his routine not mine, he yelled, and I was as clumsy as an elephant, anyway.

I knew I was not as light on my feet as Kelly, that my coffee grinders were a little bumpy and that sometimes I thumped instead of soared. Still, I never thought of myself as an elephant. "I am not clumsy," I remember defending myself with wounded pride. I didn't know what had gotten into him, but I didn't run through his number anymore whenever he was around.

Looking back now I realize how nervous Kelly must have been. Although Darlene never said, "You have to do well," I'm sure he felt he did. We both knew how hard Darlene worked for us. Kelly wanted to make her proud. He wanted to be better than good; he wanted to be discovered.

The performance was scheduled for a Sunday night. The day before, instead of regular classes, Sonny Raskin held a dress rehearsal at Hollywood High. I woke up that morning with a terrible stomachache. It was the excuse I wanted to stay home, away from my classmates all dressed up, performing on the stage without me.

Darlene, however, was not impressed. Our next-door neighbor, who took care of us after school and when Darlene went out, wasn't home, and Darlene wouldn't let me stay alone. Sick or not I had to go. Curled up in the backseat of the Disgrace, I thought about getting sick all over Kelly's costumes.

When we arrived at the auditorium Sonny Raskin was pacing back and forth between the rows of empty seats, yelling at my ballet group on the stage. We tried to slip in quietly along the far aisle, but Sonny caught sight of us.

"You," he barked. We all stopped in our tracks. "You, Margaret Muldaur." He pointed at me. "Do you know how to be a honeybee?"

I knew the part as well as I knew Kelly's. We had practiced it for weeks in class. I nodded, too scared to do anything else.

"Then get right up there on the stage and be one. Mary Lou Mizer, poor child, has come down with chicken pox."

"But I—I don't have a costume," I stammered.

"Never mind that. You can borrow Mary Lou's. Now quick, quick, buzz, buzz, fly up there. I can't have a flower without a bee. It ruins my symmetry."

Even though my stomach was churning, I wasn't going to give Sonny Raskin a chance to change his mind. I leaped up on the stage and took Mary Lou Mizer's place among the others.

I had to dance without a costume and in my bare feet because I'd left my ballet slippers at home. I doubt, however, that I disgraced the honeybees. If I saw the dance of the honeybees today, I'd probably think it was pretty dumb, but at that moment our number seemed almost as dazzling a piece of choreography as Gene Kelly's "Good Mornin'."

"Soft landings," Sonny kept reminding us. "Remember, bees fly, they flutter. They don't hop like frogs. Lightly, lightly . . ."

By the second run-through, my stomachache had miraculously disappeared.

"All right, very nice, very nice, children," Sonny finally pronounced, satisfied, or at least resigned. "Now be sure to get a good night's sleep tonight and to dream of bees and flowers. And be here on time tomorrow."

Then it was Kelly's turn. "Loosen up, Kelly. This is supposed to be fun, not punishment," Sonny called to him after he'd tapped his way through his solo. The second time around Kelly looked even worse. I had seen him do it better hundreds of times at home. Now he looked as stiff as the Tin Man.

Before we left the rehearsal, Sonny took Darlene aside and had a few words with her. I guessed it was about my costume, but I didn't have a chance to ask, for Darlene kept up a steady stream of conversation with Kelly, talking about everything except the recital. If she was trying to take Kelly's mind off the show, it didn't work too well. The more Darlene talked, the quieter Kelly became. I was so excited by my own good luck, though, that I really didn't think much about Kelly.

On our way home we picked up Mary Lou Mizer's costume. Poor Mary Lou. Before the chicken pox I had never really liked her, but her illness had suddenly turned her into one of my best friends. Unfortunately, her yellow tutu was at least two sizes bigger than I was. Because it had to be returned to her, Darlene couldn't alter it, so she pinned it to my leotard instead. Mary Lou's cloth wings were also made for a bigger bee. Fastened to my back, they stuck out like the wings of a giant moth. And no matter how Darlene shifted the headpiece with its stuffed antennae, my red hair kept showing through. When Kelly saw me, he said that I looked more like a Martian than a bee. I was too happy to even care.

That night neither Kelly nor I got much sleep. Each of us tossed and turned on opposite sides of the room.

"You scared?" he finally asked.

"A little," I said, "but more excited, like Christmas Eve. I can hardly wait until tomorrow."

"I wish I wasn't in this," he said glumly.

"Why? You're so good."

"I feel sick," he mumbled, and suddenly rushed into the bathroom. Soon I heard Darlene's footsteps and then Kelly following her into her bedroom. When Darlene looked in on me, I shut my eyes and pretended to be asleep. I didn't know if Kelly had eaten something bad, or if he'd caught something from me. Either way I was glad to be sleeping by myself.

If you've never been backstage before a musical recital with a cast of ninety kids, then there's no way I can describe the scene to you. The only other experience I've had that comes close to it was a food fight at the junior high school cafeteria, but that only lasted a few minutes before the teachers stopped it. The backstage bedlam at Hollywood High went on for almost an hour—people shouting, kids crying (ruining their makeup), desperately looking for safety pins, or ballet slippers, or parts of their costumes they'd left at home. A few, all sealed into their costumes, finally realized they had to go to the bathroom after all. When the auditorium lights dimmed, though, and the pianist began to play, backstage was magically transformed. It was as if the cast had suddenly become different people. We all lined up quietly for our entrances.

Sonny had arranged the program to open and close with the more experienced dancers. My ballet class was fifth; Kelly's numbers were third and seventh. Even in his makeup he looked ghostly as he waited in the wings for his cue. "Break a leg," I whispered.

From where I stood I couldn't see how he did when his moment finally came, but the applause seemed enthusiastic.

"How was it?" I asked, as he rushed off the stage.

"Just my solo left," he replied. "Gotta change."

Waiting for the next number—the one before mine—to finish, I felt shaky for the first time. Butterflies fluttered furiously in my stomach and my legs suddenly felt weak and wobbly. I clutched the arm of Henriette Winkler, the flower in front of me. Henriette clutched back.

Then somewhere behind me, I heard Jennifer's firm command: "All right, honeybees, fly." The next moment I was standing in the bright lights, staring out into the darkened auditorium and flapping my wings in time to the music. I couldn't make out any faces, but I could feel eyes watching me.

In the excitement of being onstage I forgot all about being afraid. Instead, I concentrated on the lyrics of our song:

"As you see, we are the honeybees.
From flower to flower we fly with ease,
Sucking nectar with our tongues,
Making honey, yum, yum, yum."

I stuck out my tongue and rubbed my stomach at all the right places in the music. Then I swarmed with the other bees to a corner, where we continued to flap our wings as the flowers entered from the opposite side.

"We are the flowers as you see
Waiting to be pollinated by the bees.
We're always happy they buzz by
Because they help us multiply."

When the flowers had finished their entrance and assumed their proper positions, we bees began to buzz around them. I had done my dance steps for weeks—they were as familiar to me as my Super Kid role or Kelly's solo—but that night I felt as if I were discovering them for the first time. It didn't matter that my costume was too big, or that I may have looked like a Martian. From the moment I was onstage, I felt like I could almost fly.

"Oh, yessiree, we are the bees.
We love to dance in the breeze
Telling others where to meet us
To find flowers that are sweetest."

Each of us then did a brief duet with our flower, then everyone danced together in a grand finale, which was the final verse of the song.

"As you see we are the honeybees.
We are the flowers if you please.
Without flowers there'd be no honey for our hive
Without bees we flowers wouldn't survive."

The number ended, we took our bows. Although the audience burst into applause, the cheering hardly mattered to me—I just wanted the dancing and the good feeling to continue. After the curtain dropped and the others scurried from the stage, I took my time.

Suddenly the curtain lifted again. Unfortunately, I was the only one left for a second bow. With no one to follow, I didn't know what to do, so I did the first thing that came to mind: a few quick shuffle steps of Kelly's routine. To my horror the audience responded with a roar of laughter. Bolting from the stage, I wished that I had caught the chicken pox instead of Mary Lou.

ON THE ROAD TO FAME
AND FORTUNE

Embarrassed by my impromptu curtain call, I waited after the show for Sonny Raskin to yell at me ("Who *ever* told you to do *that?*"). To my surprise, however, he patted me on the head. "A regular showstopper," he declared. To Kelly, he said nothing.

"What did you do?" Kelly asked sourly.

"Oh, nothing." I didn't want to talk about it.

"Meg was just her usual exuberant self," said Darlene, who was the first mother backstage to congratulate her stars.

"You mean she did something really dumb?"

"Not at all. Your sister was charming, and so were you." She put her arm around Kelly and gave him a squeeze. "I'm so proud of both of you," she went on, draping her other arm around me. She was as excited as if she had been in the show herself.

While she took turns hugging us, a stylish, slender woman a few years older than Darlene approached us. She had lavender nails and matching eye shadow and wore as much jewelry as Darlene's rich customers at Bullock's. "Adorable, adorable," she pronounced, looking us over as if we were dolls in a toy store. Then she stuck out her hand, jingling several gold bracelets. "Rhonda Cohen," she declared.

Darlene was momentarily speechless. Still dazzled, she shook Rhonda's hand automatically and introduced us to her.

"How old are you, Margaret?" Rhonda asked as she firmly gripped my hand.

"Almost six."

"Excellent," she said, as if that was the best age in the world to be. "I haven't seen you anywhere before, have I?"

I didn't know what she meant.

"Television, stage, screen, magazines, catalogs," she rattled off the list.

"This is Meg's debut," Darlene said proudly.

"Then I assume she has no representation yet."

Now Darlene looked confused.

"Has she an agent yet?" Rhonda explained.

"Oh, no, we have no agent yet," Darlene said eagerly.

"Good." Rhonda snapped open her purse and handed Darlene one of her cards. "I've been representing children for ten years now. You can ask anyone about me. I'm one of the best. Your daughter has wonderful energy. If you're interested, I'm almost certain I can get her work. I've been looking for a six-year-old redhead with personality for a while now. The last one I had grew up."

"I'm interested in finding an agent for both my children," Darlene said. I was shocked by her boldness.

Rhonda glanced at Kelly again, as if giving him a second appraisal.

"How old are you, young man?"

"I'll be seven in a week."

"Very good," she replied. Apparently being seven was not quite as good as being almost six, but it was still all right. "Yes, I'm definitely interested in both your children." Rhonda smiled and tucked her purse under her arm. "I hope to be seeing you soon. Don't wait too long to call. There are parts I could be sending them up for tomorrow. . . ." Then she was off, leaving a scented trail behind her.

"It looks like Meg has been discovered," Kelly said, sounding surprised.

"She wants to see *both* of you," Darlene answered, giving him another squeeze.

"I don't like her," he said.

I didn't agree. I was kind of dazzled, too.

"She's a very important agent," Darlene said firmly, "one of the best. . . ."

The following Saturday was our appointment with Rhonda. There were no dance lessons that day because of the recital the previous week, so we were scheduled for a morning visit. Rhonda's offices were located in a high-rise building on Sunset Boulevard in a different part of Hollywood than Sonny's studio. There were no bums sleeping in the doorways here.

The waiting room of Rhonda's office had soft, thick carpets and the kind of fancy furniture they featured in Bullock's catalogs; there was even a table full of expensive-looking toys that I knew cost a fortune. You could tell that Rhonda was pretty successful. The office was crowded with other parents and children waiting to see her, and the receptionist was so busy answering the phones that she barely had time to get your name.

The week before, Darlene tried to make our meeting with Rhonda seem like an everyday event, but both Kelly and I knew it was important that we impress this lady. Friday night Darlene had washed our hair and cut and cleaned our fingernails. For this big occasion, she also bought a dress for me and slacks and a sweater for Kelly.

When we entered the waiting room we found other children as dressed up as we were. Everyone sat stiffly on the plush furniture, ignoring the toys and magazines, and stared at the large color photographs on the walls. I recognized almost all the faces from ads on TV.

Finally we were led into Rhonda's private office. You could

smell her perfume as you entered the room, but that day her nails and matching eye makeup were green. The walls of the place were peach and the chairs and couches dark blue. Obviously she didn't like things drab.

Rhonda saw the three of us together for a few minutes. Then, while Darlene filled out long forms for us, listing everything from our athletic skills to our allergies, she talked to Kelly and me separately. Rhonda was all business.

"Why do you want to be in commercials?" she asked me without so much as a how-are-you.

"To make money," I said honestly.

Rhonda nodded as if that made sense to her, too. "Do you like to dress up, pretend to be other people?" she asked.

"Sure, all the time."

"Who do you pretend to be?"

"My favorite movie stars." I ran through a verse of "Good Mornin'." Since she seemed to like that, I did my imitation of Julie Andrews in *Mary Poppins,* and then my impression of Sonny Raskin demonstrating how to be a bee.

"Oh, you're going to love this business, Meg," she laughed.

I hadn't thought much about what doing commercials would be like, but the way Rhonda described it—"someone paying you to play make-believe"—certainly sounded like fun. After all, I did it all the time with no pay. The more she talked, the more I liked the idea of being discovered.

The only part of the interview I felt bad about was when Rhonda asked how my father felt about my acting. I had to tell her about his leaving and all. Afterward, I thought maybe I shouldn't have said so much, but I didn't want to lie about it either.

After she'd talked to me for a while she called Kelly and Darlene back in. "You have delightful children," she said to Darlene. "I'd like very much to represent them both."

Kelly didn't seem that excited but Darlene looked at us and beamed. I was feeling pretty good myself.

Then Rhonda gave Darlene "a little talk about the business." I didn't pay much attention, but I've heard Rhonda's "talk" often enough since that I know what she must have said.

"Accepting your children as clients is no guarantee that they'll get work. I don't need to tell you that this is a fiercely competitive business. Every year there are about fifteen thousand jobs for children in TV commercials—that includes babies as well as teenagers—but there are at least forty thousand cute kids out there competing for them. The fact is cuteness, like puppies, always sells soda pop and there's a lot of soda pop in the world to sell.

"No matter how cute or talented your kids are, though, they won't get all the parts they try out for. In fact, they won't get most of them—not because they performed badly or weren't good enough, but because the director or the advertisers were looking for something else. Meg has green eyes and red hair. This week, however, they may want green eyes and purple hair; next week maybe they'll want purple eyes and green hair. Who knows? There's nothing wrong with red hair and green eyes or blond hair and blue eyes. Only that's not what they're buying this week."

Finishing up, she surely mentioned her famous Rolodex. "I have three hundred names in my Rolodex, all ages, all sizes, all colors. Usually somebody I represent is right for every casting call I get, yet not always. I don't have anyone with purple hair, for instance. If that becomes popular, though, I assure you I'll get someone. But that's not your problem, that's mine. . . ."

After Rhonda finished her speech, she turned her attention back to Kelly and me. I remember her coming over to the couch, sitting down between us, and talking to us in that very serious tone that adults often use when they want to tell you something "very important."

"Do you know the yellow brick road in *The Wizard of Oz?*" she asked us.

We both nodded.

"Well, the road to fame and fortune in Hollywood is very much like it," she said. "To get your reward you need the brains of the Straw Man, the courage of the Lion, the heart of the Tin Man, and the magic of the Wizard. Naturally, it doesn't hurt to have the talent of Judy Garland, either. Yet even if you have all those things, no one can promise that you'll get what you want. So all you can do is try your best and be yourself. If you remain your fresh, natural, sparkling selves, I know you'll do just fine."

Then she let us pick a lollipop from a big glass jar on her desk and sent us on our way.

"Well, what do you think?" Darlene asked as soon as we were in the car.

Kelly was not so sure. "Are we really going to make a lot of money?" he asked.

"We'll have to see," Darlene said, "but it's possible."

"Well, then I want a new bike, and my own TV set, and a puppy—a Saint Bernard," he insisted.

"Let's wait and see what happens." Darlene laughed.

"It has to be a color TV set, too," Kelly added. If he was going to have to work, he wasn't going to do it for nothing.

"Of course," she agreed, winking at me.

"And what do you want, Meg?" she asked.

"I'm not sure," I said. "I guess I want to be a star."

HOLLYWOOD DANCE STUDIOS

ballet   tap   jazz
From beginners to the stars

Dear Mrs. Muldaur:

It has been almost a year since I have had the pleasure of seeing your delightful children at my studio. I miss their shining faces. As you know, I think both of them have promise.

Jennifer has told me that they have found success in the world of commercials. I am not surprised to hear it, but I am personally disappointed that it has cut short their dance training.

As I have said many times before, dance is the best discipline in the world. It is not only a physical but also a mental discipline. The best dancers are invariably the best students in school. I strongly believe dance should be a part of every child's development.

Success in television commercials, I'm afraid you'll find, is as short-lived as the warranties on many of the products your children are undoubtedly selling. Dance training is for life. I hope you will find time in their busy schedules to resume their lessons.

In the meantime I would appreciate it, as a personal favor to me, if you could send me their autographed pictures for my studio.

Hoping to see you again soon.

Sonny Raskin

BARBECUE GRILLS AND STAIN REMOVERS

Rhonda had warned us about the qualities we would need to succeed in show business. Unfortunately she had failed to list another essential: money. In Hollywood the road to fame and fortune was paved with many expenses along the way. Before we could even look for work, Kelly and I had to have our pictures taken by a professional photographer and hundreds of composite photographs printed.

A composite was what Rhonda sent to casting directors and advertising agencies to try to interest them in hiring us. On the front of the composite was an 8-by-11-inch head shot, on the back four smaller photographs of different poses. As with everything else, Rhonda had definite ideas about composites. "Variety and personality," she stressed, "but no animals. I can't stand animals on composites, and for godsakes don't show them on roller skates if they can't skate or in a bathing suit if they can't swim."

The photographs she picked for Kelly's composite showed him riding a bicycle, dancing, hanging from a jungle gym, and looking sad. "I look goofy there," Kelly said when he saw the picture.

"Not at all," Rhonda disagreed. "It's a lovely, pensive shot. Very soulful." The picture stayed.

The pictures she chose of me showed me hugging a doll (I rarely played with them), jumping rope, eating an apple, and looking sassy. The photographer had caught me sticking my tongue out at Kelly during the shooting and had snapped the picture. Rhonda loved it. "Now that's personality," she said.

When the completed composites arrived from the printer in June, I had to admit they looked pretty good. They must have been pretty expensive, though, because for the next few weeks we practically lived on macaroni and cheese. We even had to give up dancing lessons, but now that we had been taken on as clients of the Rhonda Cohen Agency, Darlene didn't seem to think they were quite so important anymore.

A few weeks after we got our pictures, just after school finished for the year, Rhonda started sending us out on calls. A few of them were on weekends, but most of them were during the week, which meant that Darlene had to skip work to take us around. Sometimes she'd trade hours with her friends at Bullock's; sometimes she'd just call in sick. Whatever she worked out, it was always a hassle.

The first commercial I tried out for was for a new cereal I will not name. Rhonda told Darlene it was something I might be right for, so we went. We had trouble finding the street where the casting agency was located and arrived a little late. By then the line outside the agency was already a block long. As we walked past the other mothers and their kids, all my age or a few years older, I noticed that none of them looked friendly.

It took at least an hour before my turn came. The grown-ups sat in the hall while the kids were called in, in groups of three. When they signaled us, two other girls and I entered a bare, brightly lit room where several people sat waiting in canvas chairs. A videotape camera was set up on a tripod at one end of the room. It was pointed at a long card table at the other end, where they told us kids to sit. In front of each of us was a plastic spoon and a paper bowl. A young woman came around and filled the bowls with cereal and milk. Then, on cue, we were each supposed to announce our name and the name of our agent, take a spoonful of cereal, and show how delicious it was.

"This is a great cereal, kids, so I want you to look that way," the director coached us.

I was at the far end of the table, so I had a chance to watch the other girls before they taped me. They both gave big, fake smiles. Cereal was not my favorite food, but I figured I could pretend better than that. When I tasted it, though, it was so sickeningly sweet, so gross, that I nearly gagged. I gulped and swallowed, then tried to look pleased, but I'm sure my grin was pretty sorry.

"If they can't stand cereal, I don't know why their agents send them out on this," I heard one of the women in the canvas chairs mutter.

"Thanks. That will be all, girls," the director dismissed us.

"How did it go?" Darlene asked eagerly as we left the building.

"Okay, I guess," I said, but I felt awful. My first audition, and I had blown it completely.

With Kelly, things went better. The second time out he got a job. The commercial was for barbecue grills—"Even Dad can't spoil it, if he charbroils it." Kelly's role was classified as "extra (or 'atmosphere') work" because he didn't have a speaking part. All he had to do was take a bite of the hamburger grilled in the "backyard" by his "father" and look delighted, the same "bite 'n smile" that I had messed up so badly.

Fifty boys showed up for the casting call, but Kelly got the part because he best matched the actor cast as the father. In the beginning things worked out like that for Kelly. Sometimes it seemed as if all he had to do to get hired was show up at an audition.

Although the barbecue spot only lasted thirty seconds, shooting took all day. By the time Darlene brought Kelly home, he had a stomachache from eating too many burnt burgers. "You're never supposed to eat while you're shooting," Rhonda advised him the next day. "You're just supposed to take a bite and spit it out." Still, the bellyache seemed worth it—Kelly had broken into the business and was now a professional. Rhonda's strategy, Darlene explained, was to start us on atmosphere work to give us experience in front of the cameras. Then she'd "upgrade" us to principal roles. With Kelly, at least, it seemed to be working.

Within a month he had a second job, this one for a blue jeans commercial for Japanese television. "American kids sell in Japan even better than Japanese cars sell here," Rhonda told Darlene. Kelly didn't speak in this ad either, but he got to dance in a chorus line of blue-jeaned American boys.

By Kelly's third job—flying a kite on the beach as background for a sunglasses commercial—I had tried out for nine parts and gotten none. At the Hollywood Dance Studios one case of chicken pox was enough to put me onstage, but at casting calls it looked like I would need an epidemic before I got a part. Rhonda had said that I would love the business; however, I didn't know how I'd be able to if the business didn't love me.

The funny thing was Kelly wasn't that thrilled about his success. He confided to me that he'd much rather spend his summer at day camp than standing in line for hours waiting for a chance to smile at a casting director. He said he'd even rather be dancing at Sonny Raskin's, although ever since the recital he'd become much more interested in baseball. Still, he liked getting the parts, and he liked the money he was earning. And when the chance came for him to smile for the casting director, he put everything into it.

Going to the casting calls, it was easy to see why Rhonda had decided to represent Kelly. He looked like most of the other boys who came to the auditions, only handsomer. He had, as I overheard Rhonda say to Darlene, "blendability." With his blue eyes and blond wavy hair, he fit in every place. He looked right eating hamburgers in the backyard or cereal at the breakfast table (he even liked it). Flying a kite was as easy for him as playing baseball. Even when he was sad, he looked "soulful."

I, on the other hand, didn't bear much resemblance to the girls I competed against. To begin with, not many had red hair and freckles. Few were chunky. (You couldn't sell soda or candy bars if you looked too fat.) None were red-haired, freckled, *and* chunky. Most of them looked like Mattel dolls. No matter how Darlene dressed me and fixed my hair, though, she could never turn me into Barbie.

I'd walk in for my audition, smile, frown, look hungry, disappointed, angry, whatever the director or advertising man asked for. Sometimes they wouldn't ask me to do anything. "I just want to look at you," one director said, circling around me as if I were a park statue and he were a pigeon. "Thank you," he said when he finished his examination. "Send the next one in, please."

"Thank you," you quickly learned, was their way of telling you they were going to use someone else.

Each time I was turned down, I felt worse. Kelly may have been a better dancer, but I thought I was as good an actor as he and a lot of the other kids I saw. Being able to act didn't seem to matter much, though, if they never gave you a chance to prove it. After my ninth audition at the end of August I decided to give up.

"I quit," I told Darlene. "No one's ever going to pick me."

After dragging me all over the city that summer without seeing any results, I think she was beginning to think the same thing. Even so, she didn't want to hear it from me. "I think we ought to talk to Rhonda about it," she suggested, immediately telephoning. Rhonda gave us an appointment for the next evening.

As usual Rhonda got right down to business. "Your mother says you want to quit, honey," she said, sitting down beside me on her blue corduroy couch.

I nodded. "You made a mistake when you chose me," I said. "Nobody else wants me."

"I know it's hard," she said sympathetically. "This is a tough business to crack. But I think it's just a matter of time. I know you'll get something soon."

"I don't think so. I'm not like Kelly. I'm not blendable."

Rhonda gave Darlene a sharp look. "Where did you get an idea like that, honey?" she asked me.

"I don't look like the other girls."

"You're every bit as pretty as they are," Darlene tried to reassure me. But I knew it wasn't true.

"I don't want to go to any more auditions," I said. "They're not any fun."

There was a moment's silence. Darlene watched Rhonda, waiting.

"You're right, honey," Rhonda finally said, much to Darlene's surprise. "Your brother's looks are all-American apple pie. Yours aren't. You're different, a spice-of-life kid. Your brother blends, you stand out. That's what attracted me to you. There's something special about you. It may take awhile for other people to recognize that, but I'm betting that eventually they will, and when they do your career is going to take off."

Maybe Rhonda's confidence reassured Darlene, but it didn't make me feel much better. The only product I could imagine them hiring me to sell was a diet candy bar especially made for red-headed kids.

Rhonda stood up and I could tell a speech was coming. "I've been thinking about this ever since you called," she said to Darlene. "Why haven't I been able to sell your daughter? After ten years in the business I trust my instincts. Still, I have to admit — something's not working. Then"—she snapped her fingers—"I suddenly realized why. I've been trying to sell Meg the wrong way."

She turned to me. "It's not your looks that are going to get you work. It's your personality. I've made a mistake in starting you off looking for atmosphere work. It's hard to shine where you can't speak. From now on I'm only going to send you up for speaking roles. When you have raspberries, you can't sell them like apples."

She rummaged around her desk, came up with a breakdown—a sheet listing casting requirements—for a new stain remover commercial. "Here, I want you to take her to this," she told Darlene. "I'm going to call them up and tell them you're coming, so be sure and be there on time."

Darlene rose and took the casting sheet as if it were the answer to all my difficulties. Then Rhonda offered me another of her awful lollipops and led us to the door.

"All you have to do, Meg, is be your fresh, natural self," she said. "Remember, it's make-believe, fun, pretend. I know this is going to work. Rhonda Cohen does not pick losers."

At the door she gave me a quick hug. "Thanks for coming by, sweetheart. Whenever you have a problem, I want you to feel free to bring it to me. That's what I'm here for."

I left her office not sure quite what had happened. I'd come to quit, and gone home with an appointment for another audition. But Rhonda's faith did encourage me. If she believed in me that much, maybe my luck would change.

A few mornings later Darlene called in sick once again and took me to the stain remover audition. In most of the casting sessions I had been to, they called you in in groups, but for this one they interviewed you individually. When it was my turn, I walked into the room where I found a videotape camera, lights, and several people waiting for me. The casting director introduced herself and I handed her my composite. She tossed it on a large pile of photographs without even glancing at it.

"Okay, here's the situation," she explained impatiently. "You're wearing your favorite dress, right?"

I decided to follow Rhonda's advice and be myself. "No, this isn't my favorite dress. It's my mom's favorite dress. I don't like dresses very much."

The people in the room laughed. Even the casting director smiled.

"Well, pretend it's your favorite, okay? And you've just spilled a

Coke on it, or tomato juice, something you're afraid won't ever come off. You're sure your best dress is ruined. You come running to your mom—that's me—and you say, 'Mom, Mom, look what I've done. You've got to get it out. It's my favorite dress.' Can you do that?"

"Sure." I repeated the lines for her to be sure I got them right.

"Okay, lots of emotion now. You're really upset."

This was the first audition where I had a chance to do any real acting, so I thought about it for a bit. I tried to imagine what would happen if I spilled something on the dress I was wearing. I wouldn't have cared that much, but I knew it would have bothered Darlene. She had bought the dress a few weeks before, hoping that it might change my luck. "I saw it on sale and I couldn't resist," she explained. "They won't be able to turn you down in this." But, of course, they had.

"Whenever you're ready," the cameraman said.

I took my place in front of the camera and said my name and Rhonda's, as I had been instructed. "Okay, action," the casting director called. Thinking of how upset Darlene would be, I ran to the casting director, "Mom, Mom, look at what I've done . . ." Suddenly I was crying, the rest of my lines lost in tears.

"That was lovely," the casting director said.

"Super, really super," the man from the advertising agency exclaimed. He took my composite out of the pile. "We'll be calling you," he said.

I dried my eyes, not sure whether to be embarrassed or pleased by my performance. The funny thing was that I hardly ever cried.

The casting director took my hand and walked me out to the waiting room. "Your daughter is a marvelous talent, Mrs. Muldaur," she said. "We'll be in touch."

Darlene squeezed my hand. "I told you people wouldn't be able to resist that dress," she whispered to me while she fumbled for her car keys.

The other mothers all eyed us suspiciously as we walked out.

From everything they'd said, I thought for sure I'd won the part. Rhonda telephoned the next day, though, to tell us that they still hadn't made up their minds. In fact, they wanted me to return for another screen test.

On this callback I went through the scene with the actress whom they had cast as the mother. This time, because I knew my chances were better, I was a lot more nervous. And although I wore the same dress, and tried as hard as I could to imagine Darlene's gloom if I stained it, no tears came. I was sure I'd blown it.

A week passed. Still no word. School had started, but my excitement about first grade was cooled by the anxiety of waiting to hear whether I would be on national TV. Two weeks after my callback Rhonda finally telephoned: the agency wanted to see me one more time. They told her they had narrowed the choice to me and another girl. While they were leaning toward me, they were concerned about my lack of experience. Rhonda didn't say it, but I figured they were worried that I couldn't cry on cue again. I could understand that. I didn't know if I could either.

The day before the audition, Darlene was waiting for us after school.

"What's the matter?" Kelly asked. "How come you're here?"

"You sick?" I asked.

She shook her head, then blurted out the explanation. "I guess you might as well know now. I'm not going to be working at Bullock's anymore."

I knew immediately that it was our fault. Kelly knew it, too. "You miss too much work?" he asked.

She nodded. "I couldn't work out their schedule and yours."

"What are you going to do?" Kelly asked.

"Get another job, of course," she said, as if she could find one with a snap of her fingers.

"That means more macaroni and cheese, doesn't it?" he said.

"Not at all," she answered. "I've put away most of the money you earned, and that will get us through." As if to prove it, she took us out for pizza that night. That was Darlene's way. No matter how bad things got, she believed they always worked out happily in the end.

When Darlene drove me to the agency for my final screen test, I was ready. Actually, the audition wasn't that hard. All I had to think about was Darlene losing her job because of me and the tears spilled down my cheeks. To be honest, in some ways it's simpler to cry for the camera than in real life: when you're acting no one knows what you're really crying about. I left the audition feeling pretty good, proud to be able to draw tears so easily.

The next day, at recess, I saw Darlene furiously signaling me from the other side of the playground's chain-link fence. I knew at once why she had come. I ran over to her screaming, "I got it, I got it." We both jumped up and down and tried to kiss and hug each other through the wire. Everyone must have thought we were crazy.

"This is silly," Darlene finally said. "We have to act more dignified." Then she looked at me mischievously. "How would you like to play hookey today?"

I don't know what excuse she gave the principal, but fifteen minutes later I was called to his office and freed for the day. Leaving the school that morning I felt lifted from the ranks of the first grade. While my classmates were skipping rope, I had more serious concerns. I was an actress who would appear all over the country on TV. I felt terribly grown up and terribly important.

The time had come for me to do my part to keep us afloat. And I had.

NATIONAL CORNGROWERS' ASSOCIATION SPOT

FADE IN:

INTERIOR KITCHEN--DAY

A table by a window. The sunlight illuminates a
plate of golden, steaming corn on the cob.

A seven-year-old girl is seated at the table.
She picks up one of the ears and begins buttering
it, then looks up at the CAMERA.

                    GIRL
          I bet you don't know all the
          reasons I like corn.

                    OFF-CAMERA VOICE
          Because it tastes so good.

                    GIRL
               (nodding in agreement)
          Uh-huh. . .

She finishes buttering the corn.

                    OFF-CAMERA VOICE
          Because it goes with so many
          other foods.

                    GIRL
          Uh-huh. . .

She salts the corn.

                    OFF-CAMERA VOICE
          Because you can make a meal of it
          all by itself.

                    GIRL
          Uh-huh. . .

She puts some pepper on it.

                    OFF-CAMERA VOICE
          Because it's so nutritious.

                    GIRL
          Uh-huh. . .

She begins to eat the corn with relish.

                    OFF-CAMERA VOICE
          Because. . . because you can make
          popcorn from it.

The little girl gives the camera a "that's-a-dumb-
remark" look.

                    GIRL
          No, because it doesn't stick
          between my teeth.

She breaks into a huge grin clearly revealing her
two missing upper front teeth.

FREEZE-FRAME

                    OFF-CAMERA VOICE
          Corn--a vegetable for all reasons.

IN THE LAND OF SUITS
AND PONYTAILS

The stain removal commercial launched my television career, but the Corngrowers' Association spot made me a minor star. In the fall of second grade, a few months after I turned seven, I lost an upper front tooth. Darlene called Rhonda to find out where to send me to get flippers, the clip-in false teeth that kids who act in commercials wear. Even though everyone loses their baby teeth around six or seven, candy and soft drink advertisers don't like to use kids with missing front teeth. Like fat people, they might give their product a bad image.

In any case, the day Darlene telephoned, Rhonda happened to receive the breakdown for the corngrowers' spot. And when Darlene told her about my tooth, she said, "Great, how soon before she'll lose the other one?"

The second tooth was a little loose, but the advertising agency wasn't willing to wait for nature to take its course. So the day before the first callback Darlene sent me to the dentist to have it pulled. By the time I arrived for my second audition, about all I had to do was open my mouth and smile and the part was mine.

The day we shot the commercial I ate parts of seventy-nine ears of corn before everyone was finally satisfied with the results. And even though I spit a lot of that out, I don't think I ate corn again for a year afterward.

I didn't eat any macaroni and cheese either. Now that Kelly and I were working regularly, Darlene didn't have to scrimp on food anymore. In fact, we often ate out, and not just at Schwab's either. Now we could afford fancier places. In the next four years, Kelly and I appeared in over a hundred commercials, selling everything from cat food to bagels. When Darlene was first fired from Bullock's she went back to waiting on tables. Within half a year, though, we were earning enough residuals so she could give that up. Residuals are the extra payments you receive each time a spot is broadcast. You usually don't get paid that much for the day or two it takes to shoot a commercial, but if the ad is shown a lot on TV, you can make thousands, or "in five figures," as Rhonda would say.

Kelly and I never really knew how much we made. Rhonda didn't believe we should be concerned about that. "You kids just worry about the acting," she said. "I'll worry about the money." (For her worrying, of course, she got ten percent of everything we ever earned.) Still Kelly and I knew the money had to be good.

Not all the commercials we acted in were successful, of course. Sometimes, after they were finished, the company or the advertising agency decided they didn't like them and never aired them. But other ads, especially for soap and toothpaste, played over and over again throughout the country. The corngrowers' commercial was one of those. They ran it for over a year, and each time it appeared I made money, around $20,000 in all, I think. I figured it out recently and that's more than $250 for each ear of corn I bit into.

Even though Kelly and I earned all this money ourselves, it didn't all go to us. After Rhonda's cut, Darlene put a part of it in a trust fund for us that we couldn't touch until we were eighteen. The rest she kept for living expenses. Since it was clear we could make so much more than she, Darlene gave up trying to hold down a job. Besides, driving us from audition to audition, and taking us to the set whenever we had a part, was full-time work, anyway.

Just before I started third grade, Darlene moved us out of the crowded two-bedroom apartment in Culver City to a three-bedroom house in Studio City, a neighborhood in the Valley, just north of Hollywood. Darlene picked the area because the schools were good and she wanted a house with a backyard where she could grow roses and Kelly could keep a dog. Darlene refused to buy him a Saint Bernard but compromised on a cocker spaniel, which Kelly named Bernie. The same year Darlene also sold the Disgrace for scrap and bought a new Volvo station wagon. If you looked at us from the outside, with our neat rented house and trim lawn, our station wagon in the driveway and Bernie barking in the backyard, we looked just like every other family on the block.

It's not the way Kelly and I felt, however. We knew we were different from the other kids in our neighborhood, and they knew it, too. There was no professional school for kid actors in L.A., so we had to go to public school like everyone else. Our absences, however, were frequent. Usually we missed at least one day a week and sometimes more. Even when we did go to school, we didn't have much chance to play afterward, for we were generally rushing to another audition. Since I liked reading and was pretty good at math, I didn't have much trouble keeping up with the work, but all those missed days and auditions definitely made me, and Kelly, outsiders.

When kids saw us on TV, they'd hound us with smart remarks. "How come you're not eating corn for lunch?" was one popular line. "Whatsamatter? Got some stuck between your teeth?" Or, "Hey, I caught you on the tube last night. You look much uglier in person." For some reason that always seemed to crack people up. After Kelly did a commercial showing how many different kinds of sandwiches you could make with cream cheese, he took a real ribbing. "Hey, Kelly Cream Cheese," the older kids called. "How about a knuckle-sandwich? Or doesn't that go good with cream cheese?"

Secretly, though, I think they were all a little envious, for as soon as the teasing stopped, the pumping began. "You make a lot of money doing those dumb commercials, don't you?" they'd ask. "It doesn't look that hard. You don't have to act or anything. You must know somebody in the business, don't you? That's how you got in."

It was no use trying to explain to them what it was like: having to wake up at five in the morning to get to the set for a seven o'clock call; shooting in Griffith Park in a short-sleeve summer dress in freezing temperatures, or sweating for hours in a snowsuit under the hot studio lights; having to cry on cue not once, but several times, so they could film it from different angles; working with directors who screamed at you when you messed up; waiting for hours to see a casting director who would dismiss you with a glance that said, "Why-did-they-ever-send-her?"

Besides, whatever we told the other kids would never convince them that they couldn't do commercials as well as we did. And maybe they could. "You're not so special," I remember a girl telling me one day. "The only reason you got that corn commercial is because your teeth fell out."

"That's not true. I had to have them pulled," I defended myself, exaggerating a little to impress her, but it had no effect.

"Well, I bet your new ones will grow in crooked," she predicted nastily.

Until my adult teeth did come in, I worried that maybe she'd be right, that crooked teeth would be my punishment for making so much money so young. Despite the razzing of the kids, Rhonda was right, though: I loved the business, that is, once I got a part. Although a few directors treated you like the trainer at the obedience school where we took Bernie—"Stand here, look there, wait a beat, then smile"—many of them encouraged you to use your imagination and act. "Pretend you haven't had anything to eat today," a director might suggest before a fast-food commercial. Or, "Make believe it's your birthday and this is a special treat." I liked playing around that way, testing different ways to say my lines to see which sounded best. Fooling around like that during rehearsals, sometimes you'd come up with something that the director really liked.

Being able to act helped, but it didn't always get you the job. Even losing weight didn't make much difference. When a hundred pretty girls—all about the same height and shape—turn up for a ten-second nonspeaking part in a commercial, how do you decide which one is best? Often the ad people couldn't. That's why they had so many callbacks. The filmmakers, or "ponytails" as they were called because of their long hair, would blame the advertising executives. The execs, or "suits," nicknamed for their dress, would, in turn, blame the ponytails. "The ponytails have nixed red hair for this," I'd hear. Or, "The suits are looking for something more 'middle of the road.' " Sometimes there would be five or six callbacks before a choice was made. After the third callback, at least, union regulations—we were all in the actors' union—made them pay you for auditions.

Often it was difficult to see why someone won a part. Although I was pretty successful, I was passed over more than I was picked, just as Rhonda had warned. And when they did hire me, it could just as easily have been because of luck, like the time my teeth fell out, as the way I delivered my lines. Even so, when I didn't get the job, I was always sure that it was my fault, that I really didn't have any talent, that there was nothing special about me. Acting in commercials it was hard to get conceited because there was always someone waiting to reject you.

Sitting in the reception rooms before an interview was worse than facing the suits and ponytails. The kids' jealousy at school was nothing compared to the venom of stage mothers. While we waited to audition, many of the mothers would work over the competition. They would, for example, make little digs at me to

Darlene: "Isn't she too tall for this part?" or "Isn't she too old for this one?" or "That's such a beautiful dress. I hope you didn't buy it especially for this—I heard they want a more boyish look." Or cruelest of all, they would ask, "Were you at such and such a casting session last week? You weren't? Meg was exactly what they were looking for. You ought to talk to your agent about that."

The women (and an occasional man) often gathered in little groups in the agency corridors, exchanging information, comparing notes about the business, and backbiting. Sometimes, as we walked by, conversation suddenly stopped, and you would wonder if they had been gossiping about you.

Having spent hundreds of hours in the waiting rooms of ad agencies, I eavesdropped on a number of conversations. I heard parents tearing down other children and threatening their own. "You don't get a part soon and you can walk to these casting sessions," I overheard one mother say to her son, who didn't look as if he wanted to be there anyway. Not many parents threatened their kids, but most of them criticized. "Look at Meg, look at how cheerful she always is. Why don't you try being a little more like her?" Or, "Why didn't they take you? Didn't you do what you were told?" Every week you'd hear the same chorus of complaints: Don't shout. Don't pick your nails. Don't pick your nose. Don't fool with your hair. Don't fidget. Straighten up. Smooth your dress. Comb your hair. Watching the kids, you could see they had long ago stopped listening.

Some parents, desperate for their kids to succeed, would even bribe them before a casting session. "If you get this part, I'll buy you a new ten-speed," or "a stereo," or "a golden retriever." Once I even heard a father say, "Get this part and I'll put a swimming pool in the backyard." Thinking about it now, I wonder who was paying for the pool.

Darlene wasn't like the other parents, though. She didn't threaten or criticize or bribe; she didn't have to. Both Kelly and I knew the consequences of being unemployed. Neither of us wanted to go back to sharing a bedroom in Culver City. Darlene, Kelly, and I all had the same goal, so we all rooted for one another to succeed. Despite any competition for work between Kelly and me, we both knew we were on the same team. And Darlene was both our coach and our head cheerleader. In the car, on the way to casting sessions, she would sing and joke with us, and pass out sugarless gum to relax us before our interviews. If there was a script, she would always try to get it ahead of time so she could help us practice our lines. If we didn't get a part, she was always there to console us, to assure us that we would get the next one. And often enough, we did.

Dear Miss Muldaur:

I have been following your career for some time, ever since I first saw you in a commercial for Tuff Stain Remover. My two daughers, Rena and Liza, are also your fans. Every time they have seen you in a commercial, they have wanted me to buy that product.

Unfortunately, many of the products you have advertised are defective, or worse. The stain remover did not remove cherry stains from Liza's favorite blouse. The toy cake mixer you advertised last Christmas broke the first day and had to be sent back to the factory. The new one they sent us worked for only two days. We did not bother returning it.

Despite these disappointments, my daughters remained your loyal fans and urged me to buy the latest product you are selling on all the networks, Stay-Away Mosquito Repellent. When Rena tried it, however, she promptly broke out in a terrible rash on her face and arms and had to be rushed to our family doctor.

You are obviously a very talented young lady. Why waste these talents on such shoddy and dangerous goods? My daughters and I will never buy anything you advertise again.

I thank you for one thing, though. Rena's rash made me so angry that I have now joined MOMA (Mothers to Overcome Misleading Advertising). I urge your mother to join as well and put a stop to all the harm you are doing.

Indignantly yours,

Marilyn Radley

A FORK IN THE ROAD

Even with all the difficulties of working in commercials, Kelly, Darlene, and I were pretty happy. We could probably have gone on living that way a lot longer except for one thing: Kelly and I grew up.

I was eight and Kelly was nine when we moved to our house in Studio City. That year was our most successful. Kelly played in several long-running spots—for cream cheese, a computer game, and an insurance company. I won the lead part in a sixty-second soft drink ad that won several Clios (an award like an Oscar) for best commercial; the company ran it over and over again for sixteen months. We did so well that year that Darlene saved up enough money to buy the house we were renting and refurnish it.

As a reward for all our hard work, we even took a long vacation, a slow drive up the California coast to Orick, stopping at Santa Barbara, Carmel, and San Francisco along the way. Darlene only stayed a few days with Grandma before driving back to L.A., but she left Kelly and me there for three more weeks. Looking back, I don't remember anything special that we did in Orick. Not having to do anything, though, or rush anywhere, made it a real treat.

Unfortunately, as they say in the business, our profits peaked that year. After that, although Kelly and I continued going to as many auditions as before, the jobs began to fall off. The "magic years" (as Rhonda called them) for kids who acted in commercials were between ages six and ten. When you got to be ten, the suits didn't seem to think you were as charming anymore. Most of the kids in the business knew this, so they often lied about their age. I knew several who, hunching their shoulders to appear smaller, claimed to be ten when they were actually eleven or twelve.

At eleven, jobs in commercials were definitely harder to come by. All you had to do was walk into the waiting room of an audition to see your days were numbered. By the time I was ten it seemed that every time we went to a new casting session, the kids were younger. The older ones we were used to seeing gradually disappeared. Their voices and bodies changed, they got awkward and pimply, and all at once (except for acne cream commercials) they were gone, vanished.

I watched this happen with Kelly. For a half year after he turned eleven he didn't work at all. And when he finally landed a job, it was a disaster. He was chosen for a lead role in an amusement park commercial that featured him and an eleven-year-old girl on the park's major rides. It was a fun job, and after six months of not working, Kelly was looking forward to it. On the first day of rehearsal the suits discovered the girl was an inch taller than Kelly. That night Rhonda called to say that Kelly was out. He tried to be cool about it, said he had hated the girl anyway, but I could tell he was hurt. Who wouldn't be, thrown away like a pair of jeans that no longer fit?

The funny thing is, a few months later, Kelly started to shoot up like a weed. That didn't help him either, though. When he was almost twelve he auditioned for a tennis shoe commercial, for which we all thought he had a good chance. The director had worked with Kelly before on a very popular cereal ad, and he had even dated Darlene a few times. But Kelly wasn't even asked for a callback.

"What happened?" I asked him later that night.

"Nothing." He shrugged. "I didn't get it."

"But didn't Rick say anything?" I pressed him.

"Yeah, he said, 'What happened to that cute little boy I worked with a few years ago? He's the one I want for this.' "

I called Rick some names I'd learned working on film sets.

"Yeah, but it's the truth," Kelly said. "I'm not as cute as I used to be, and neither are you."

I knew that Kelly was right. Soon I would be too old to drool over cereal myself or ooh and aah over Jell-O. I worried about what would happen to us then. I knew Darlene had put some money aside "for a rainy day," but I didn't know how much or how long we could live on it if Kelly and I both stopped working. Even when we lived in Culver City, Darlene had had trouble paying all our bills on her cosmetics counter salary. If she had to go back to work, where was she going to find a job that paid enough to support us in Studio City?

Often when I worried about things like that I thought of Ryan and wondered if, by any chance, he might return for us. I knew he'd never come back for Darlene, but I thought maybe someday he'd turn on his television set in Portland, recognize Kelly or me, and realize how much he'd been missing all these years. Then he'd fly down here and take us back to Oregon with him. In the occasional birthday cards he sent us, though, he never mentioned seeing us on TV. Maybe he didn't have a set, I excused him, or maybe we had changed so much that, if he did see us, he didn't even recognize us anymore.

Another daydream I sometimes had was that Darlene would find herself another husband, preferably someone rich and handsome, who would move us all to a house on the beach at Malibu or to one perched on the top of a canyon, overlooking the city. Unfortunately, after what happened with Ryan, Darlene said she no longer wanted anything to do with marriage—not men—just marriage.

Even so, I never lost hope. "Do you ever think you're going to marry again?" I would ask as casually as possible every few months.

"Oh, maybe some day," she'd say vaguely. "Right now, though, the most important thing to me is you kids."

"But what's going to happen to you when we grow up?" I'd argue, trying to convince her of the advantage of marriage.

"Maybe by then I'll be old enough to take care of myself," she'd answer, smiling.

Although Darlene always acted optimistic about the future, I think she really worried about it as much as I did. One of Rhonda's first lessons to her, though, was not to burden us with her fears. ("Nervousness is as contagious as flu," was another of Rhonda's sayings.) So whatever concerns Darlene had, she tried hard to keep them to herself. When Kelly's career took a nose dive, though, her cheerleading began to falter. She, too, had heard Rhonda talk about the "magic years." She must have wondered if this was the beginning of the end.

After the tennis shoe disaster, Kelly refused to go to the next audition Rhonda arranged for him. "I have to go to the library to do some research for a geography report," he told Darlene, but I knew it was a lie. Whatever Darlene believed, she didn't try to change his mind. Every time Rhonda called for possible parts after that—and she didn't call often—Kelly was always ready with an excuse not to go. He didn't talk about it much to me, and he never said he was quitting the business completely, but it was pretty clear that he had.

It was easy to see he felt pretty bad about the whole thing. He'd come home after school, take Bernie for his walk, then go into his room, shut the door, turn on his TV or stereo, and not come out until dinner. After dinner he'd disappear again, hanging a DO NOT DISTURB sign on his door.

Darlene tried to cheer him up, encouraging him to go out for a few parts, to take up dance again with Sonny Raskin ("You were such a marvelous dancer. You had so much promise."), but Kelly would just walk out in mid-sentence. I understood how he felt. Even so, *I* wasn't ready to retire from show biz. What would I do if I couldn't act? Lock myself in my room like Kelly and listen to music all day? Besides, with Darlene and Kelly out of work, and no rich husband in sight, what would we do about money? I decided I needed to talk to Rhonda about my career.

"Honey, what else is an agent for?" she asked when I called. "Why don't you come over tomorrow afternoon after school?"

As soon as I walked into Rhonda's office, I told her what I'd been thinking. "I want to do more than commercials. I want to be a real actress."

"But you already are one," she protested, waving her polished nails, a new color, as usual. "True, crying over a stained dress doesn't qualify for an Academy Award or Emmy, but I certainly call it acting. Although the movie industry may not have recognized it yet, there's no doubt in my mind that you're an actress. Your brother might have had the right look, but from the moment I saw you at that dance recital, I knew you had the right instincts. I never intended to limit you to commercials. You have to go with the opportunities, though, and you must admit, you've been constantly in demand. . . ."

"Do you really think I can get roles in TV?"

"Honey, have I done all right for you up to now? TV, movies, stage, whatever you want. Just trust me. The money I expect you to make me, I'm counting on to retire."

She reached for her jar of lollipops to offer me one, then she thought better of it. Serious actresses didn't lick lollipops. They were just for kids who did commercials, who only had to "bite'n smile."

Rhonda was as good as her word. Just before summer vacation began, I got a small role in a movie of the week as a moody younger daughter in a family suffering through a divorce. The movie was much more fun than any of the commercials I had done. Darlene and I even got to fly to San Francisco to shoot some exterior scenes. We stayed overnight in a plush hotel and spent all the next day riding cable cars and sightseeing. The best part, though, was a scene I did in the studio where I got to throw a terrific tantrum and fling real plates against the wall. I got so caught up in doing it that I didn't even hear the director yell "cut." When I finished smashing the last dish on the table I looked up, out of breath, and realized that all the film crew was standing there, watching me.

"Now that's what I call a real tantrum," the director said, putting his arm around me.

"I guess I got carried away," I said, embarrassed.

"Hey, kiddo, don't let me ever catch you apologizing for a scene like that. You were splendid, full of red-haired Irish fury."

The movie role led to appearances in two short-lived weekly TV series. In one I played a battered child, in the other a real obnoxious one. "Typecasting," Kelly commented about the second. "They knew a natural brat when they saw one."

"If that's all it takes, then you could be a superstar," I replied. Since Kelly had "hung up his flippers," as he put it, we had not been getting along too well. Although he pretended not to care that I was working and he wasn't, I think he did.

Anyway, after months of hiding out in his room, he had discovered something else to do with his time—learning to smoke and hanging around the video arcades with a bunch of sixth-grade guys. They wore their shirt collars up and stuck cigarettes behind their ears. I thought they looked silly, and Darlene thought worse, but Kelly was completely loyal to them. It bothered Darlene a lot that that's how Kelly spent his time, but she didn't stop him. I guess she thought it was better than the alternatives.

Once, when he was hurrying off, I asked if he was having more fun now than before.

He thought about it a moment, then answered, "Maybe you think some of the stuff I do is dumb, but at least I'm doing it with friends. And I don't have to try out every day to hang around with them. When I was working all the time, I didn't have any friends, and neither do you."

I thought about what Kelly had said later that night as I was studying the role of Carrie in *The Kid and the Cabbie*. (Rhonda had arranged for me to read for the part and had sent the script.) I wanted to have friends my own age, too, I told myself, but if I gave up the business I wouldn't be special anymore. Even though I often felt lonely, it was comforting to know that at least I was an actress, not a nobody.

ACT ONE

SCENE THREE

EXT. RESTAURANT - DAY (CONTINUOUS ACTION)

(CARRIE BURSTS OUT OF THE RESTAURANT, HESITATES A
BEAT TRYING TO DECIDE IN WHICH DIRECTION TO FLEE,
THEN DASHES BETWEEN TWO PARKED CARS INTO THE
STREET. SHE IS IMMEDIATELY KNOCKED FLAT ON HER
BACK BY TONY'S CHECKER CAB, WHICH SWERVES SUDDENLY
TOWARD THE CURB TO PICK UP ANOTHER FARE.

A CROWD IMMEDIATELY GATHERS AROUND CARRIE,
SHIELDING HER FROM VIEW. TONY GETS OUT HIS CAB,
VISIBLY AGITATED)

                    FIRST BYSTANDER
          Hit her like a ton of bricks.

                    SECOND BYSTANDER
          Flattened her like a pancake.

                    TONY
          Hey, let me through there. I'm
          the one who hit her.

(THE CROWD PARTS TO LET HIM THROUGH. CARRIE IS
SITTING ON THE PAVEMENT LOOKING A LITTLE DAZED)

                    TONY
          You okay, kid?

                    CARRIE
          I don't know. You Saint Peter?

                    TONY

          I hate to disappoint you, kid,

          but you're still alive.

                    CARRIE

          No thanks to you.

(SHE STARTS TO GET UP)

                    FIRST BYSTANDER

(TRYING TO RESTRAIN HER)

          Don't move. Something could be

          broken.

(CARRIE GETS UP ANYWAY, ALTHOUGH WINCING A LITTLE

IN PAIN)

                    TONY

          You all in one piece, kid?

(SHE LIFTS ONE FOOT, SETS IT DOWN; IT SEEMS TO

BE ALL RIGHT. SHE LIFTS THE OTHER FOOT AND TESTS

IT WITH A SWIFT KICK TO TONY'S SHIN. TONY LETS

OUT A HOWL)

                    BYSTANDERS

(CHEERING)

          That-a-girl!

(A MAN WITH A BRIEFCASE PUSHES HIS WAY THROUGH

THE SPECTATORS)

                    LAWYER

(OUT OF BREATH)

        I was standing at the corner and

        heard the screech. I came as

        fast as I could. May I congrat-

        ulate you, young lady. Next to

        a Mercedes you've picked the best

        vehicle to get hit by in town.

        We've never lost a case against

        a taxi.

(HE HANDS CARRIE HIS CARD)

                    LAWYER (CONT'D)

        Call me in the morning. Behind

        every cloud is a silver lining.

                    TONY

(APPEALING TO THE CROWD)

        Hey, you saw it. She ran right

        into my cab. I didn't even see

        her.

                    FIRST BYSTANDER

        You bet you didn't.

                    SECOND BYSTANDER

        Flattened her like a pancake.

                    CARRIE

(LOOKING AT THE CARD)

          You mean I could sue for this?

                    LAWYER

          It's one of the great virtues of

          the American legal system.

(AT THAT MOMENT THE MANAGER AND A WAITRESS EMERGE

FROM THE RESTAURANT AND SPOT CARRIE)

                    WAITRESS

(POINTING)

          That's her. She's the one who

          didn't pay.

                    CARRIE

          Cripes!

(SHE STARTS LIMPING AWAY)

                    MANAGER

          Stop, thief!

(HE AND THE WAITRESS START RUNNING AFTER HER)

                    FIRST BYSTANDER

          How do you like that?

                    LAWYER

          In this country even a thief has

          the right to sue.

(HE WALKS AWAY)

                        SECOND BYSTANDER

(ADDRESSING TONY)

          Are you going to let her get away

          with that? She walked right into

          your car...could have wrecked it.

          I'd flatten the kid.

(TONY GLARES AT THE SECOND BYSTANDER. HE RUBS HIS

LEG AND STARES OFF IN THE DIRECTION CARRIE HAS

FLED)

CUT TO:

THE DIFFERENCE
BETWEEN BMWS AND
ROLLS ROYCES

I read three times for the part of Carrie, the last with Wallace Snyder, for whom the series and the role of Tony had been specially created. I had seen Wallace a number of times before on TV and was very nervous before my audition with him.

He was in his late fifties now but had been a star since Darlene was a kid. In the shows that I had seen him in he played the same kind of character, a surly, rumpled grouch who was always scattering his cigar ashes on the furniture and insulting other people. I wondered if he was like that in real life.

When Darlene and I entered the Burbank studio where the reading for the pilot of the series was to be taped, Wallace was, in fact, slouched in a director's chair sprinkling his cigar ashes on the floor. He switched his cigar to the other hand long enough to shake mine.

"So you want to be an actress, young lady?" The way he said it sounded like a dare.

"Yes, I would." I tried to act more confident than I felt.

"Well, we'll soon see." He picked up the script on his lap and settled back into his chair. He said nothing further to me, so I just tried to study my part, too.

In the pilot Carrie runs away from her foster family—the third for that year—in Bakersfield, a small town in central California. She has just enough money to buy a bus ticket to L.A. and arrives there with only a dollar in her pocket and her wits. Famished, she stops at a restaurant and orders a large meal, then slips out without paying. As she runs across the street, she is promptly hit by Tony's cab. Feeling guilty about the accident, and worried that Carrie's family will sue him, Tony pays for her meal at the restaurant and takes her to the hospital for X-rays. By the end of the pilot, after Carrie and Tony have traded pages and pages of insults, Carrie has found a new home, one that everyone connected with the show hoped would last for several seasons.

When it came time to read through our scenes together, I found it easy to play opposite Wallace. I didn't have to try to know how Carrie felt: I was furious at his coldness toward me. The only tough scene was the last one in which Carrie agrees to stay with him for a while. When I read the script over I wasn't sure why Carrie would do that, after the way Tony had treated her. Then I thought maybe she stayed because she had no place else to go, so that's the way I played it, as if tomorrow she might change her mind and run away again. It was exactly how I felt about the show at the moment. I knew it was a good opportunity, but I didn't know if I wanted to work with Wallace week after week.

When we had finished our reading and Lou Fleisher (the show's creator and executive producer) and the others were talking, Wallace came over to me. "Well, kid, I'm not the producer, but for my money you've got the part. The only thing is next time you kick me, you've got to learn to do it easier." He grinned, or at least I thought he did—it vanished so quickly I couldn't be sure—shoved his cigar back in the corner of his mouth and walked away. I looked around for Darlene and saw her talking to Lou. From the glow on her face, I knew that Carrie was mine.

Driving home, neither Darlene nor I said very much. I think we were both too much in shock to be excited. Nevertheless we stopped off at HäagenDazs for ice-cream sundae to celebrate.

It was a very quiet celebration. I was happy about getting the part but a little scared about the changes it would bring. If the show went on the air in the fall, it would mean a whole new life for me. No more rushing to auditions after school, but no more school either. I knew I wouldn't miss commercials or Carpenter Elementary for that matter, but I didn't know what it would be like working five days a week and taking classes on the set. It was like moving to a new city that you'd only visited for a few hours once before.

"Well, here's to Carrie." Darlene raised her water glass as a toast. We clinked our glasses together and drank in silence.

"You know you really were terrific," she said as if she couldn't quite believe it herself.

"You really think so?" I asked. To keep up our confidence she was always telling Kelly and me how good we were.

"Absolutely," she said. "Watching you tonight there were a few moments I almost forgot you were my daughter. When I was your age . . . oh, how I wished I could be a movie star. I'd spend hours in front of the mirror, one week trying to look like Julie Christie, the next week like Julie Andrews. I could never make up my mind which one I wanted to be. Of course I couldn't be either. The difference between us, Meg, is that you have what I didn't— talent. I could never transform myself into a character the way you do."

It made me sad to hear her say those things. "Oh, Carrie and I aren't that much different," I said. "You're the one who's always saying the line between bright and bratty is very thin." I grinned.

She smiled back. "We'll see how many of Carrie's lines you try to use at home."

A few days later, after Lou and Rhonda had settled on my pay for appearing in the pilot, Lou invited Darlene and me to lunch at La Serre, a very expensive French restaurant in Studio City. The place itself was very fancy. Designed like a patio garden, it had brick floors and was divided into smaller sections by white trellises covered with hanging plants and flowers. The tables were set with heavy silver plates and china in a pretty flower pattern. When the waiter handed me my menu, I couldn't find any prices on it. I peeked at Darlene's and saw that hers was the same. Later she told me La Serre was the sort of high-toned restaurant where only the men got menus with prices. Women weren't supposed to worry about how much the food cost, they were just supposed to enjoy it.

It was hard to enjoy the food, though, when I couldn't even read the menu. Everything was in French and nothing looked familiar. When I asked Lou to order for me, he recommended the *bifteck bearnaise*, which turned out to be a hamburger with a terrible sauce (most of which I managed to scrape off when no one was looking). Soon, though, even I realized that the food wasn't the real reason why we were there. La Serre was filled with a lot of show biz people and network bigwigs, and Lou wanted to introduce us to them. In fact, he pulled so many people over to our table as they passed by that my French hamburger got cold long before I could finish it.

Lou said pretty much the same thing to all of them: "Do you remember Margaret O'Brien? Well, I want you to meet her modern namesake, Margaret O'Brien Muldaur. You're going to be seeing a lot of this kid." Or, "I want you to meet the Tatum O'Neal of the eighties," or "the Kristy McNichol." He kept trying out different comparisons. The more he said about me, the worse I began to feel. What if I didn't turn out to be like any of those other stars? By the end of lunch I was feeling so sick that I passed up the great-looking pastry they served for dessert.

I didn't listen to a lot of what Lou said, but I do remember his words about the odds of producing a successful TV show. Every year, he explained, writers and producers would pitch at least 2,500 ideas for new shows to a network. Of those ideas maybe one hundred twenty-five would be developed into scripts, thirty to thirty-five made into pilots, four aired. One might survive for a second season. "But if that show goes," he said, "you hit the jackpot."

"The difference between a pilot and a series, moneywise . . ." He searched for a good example. "Well, it's the difference between owning a BMW and a Mercedes. The difference between a series that goes a year, and one that's renewed for a second or third season, well that's the difference between a Mercedes and a Rolls. But if the series goes five or six years, long enough to establish a real following and to build up a big supply of programs, then when it finishes running on the network, it can be resold to individual stations and run again in the afternoons. Then you're not talking about cars anymore. Then you're talking about buying yourself a Lear jet."

"I'd be happy just to get a new bike," I told him. Lou and Darlene both laughed. I didn't really see that much difference between a BMW and a Rolls, but I didn't say so, because to Lou there was obviously a big one.

"If this series is the hit I think it's going to be," he said, "by the time you are driving, you'll be able to buy whatever kind of car you want."

So far, however, the network had only ordered a pilot. I went home that afternoon and tried not to think about anything that Lou had said. It was hard, though, not to worry. What if Lou had made a terrible mistake and I turned out to be a big flop? What if the show failed because of me?

The first day of rehearsal I had as many butterflies as I did when I auditioned with Wallace. I think even Lou was nervous, too, for he gathered all the cast and crew together for a little pep talk. "In the twelve years I've written for television, I've worked with some very talented people," he said, "but I can honestly say—and this is not something I'd ever tell your agents—that never before have I worked with a group as talented as this. The truth. No hype." He crossed his heart. "And the reason I know it's true is that I hand-picked every one of you. Everyone on this show is a winner. Every-one. And since all of you are winners, the show can't help but be a winner, too. It's that simple. The only rule I know for success on TV is having the best talent around, and you're the best."

I wanted to believe him, but since Lou's powers of exaggeration were legendary, it was hard to trust him.

He went on to introduce the other "winners" of his "creative team"—his co-producer, the director, two other writers, and the cast. Besides Wallace and myself, there were three other main characters: Mort Stein, Monica Hale, and Sandra Darling. Mort played another cabbie, Punch Drabkin, Wallace's best friend. Wallace was tall and lanky and Mort short and stout, so they looked funny just standing next to each other. Monica Hale was a very handsome woman in her late forties, a stage actress from New York who had come to L.A. especially for the show. She played Alexandra Hill, the snobbish divorcee who lived in the apartment above Wallace and who was trying to save enough money to move to a better neighborhood. Sandra Darling, who was a year older than I was, played Monica's beautiful and uppity daughter, Olivia.

Sandra was Lou's personal discovery. He had seen her in a play at the private school she attended and asked her to try out for *The Kid and the Cabbie*. She must have been exactly what he had in mind, for as soon as she read for him, he offered her the role of Olivia. It was her first professional job and she was as excited as I remember being at Sonny Raskin's recital. "Do you think we'll see Matt Dillon eating lunch at the commissary?" she whispered to me during Lou's pep talk.

That first rehearsal I thought I'd probably hate Sandra as much as I was supposed to in the show, but by the end of the week we spent shooting the pilot, I'd changed my mind. Sandra was differ-ent from any of the kids I had worked with before. For one thing, since her father was a rich attorney, she didn't really need the job. In fact, at first her parents had even refused to let her take it. "I had to pout and carry on *two* whole weeks before Mummy finally got Daddy to change his mind," she told me. "He still thinks that television is a 'morally dubious environment.' " I wasn't sure exactly what "morally dubious" meant, but it sounded just like the kind of snotty remark that Lou would write for Sandra in the script. In many ways, I guess, she was like her character in the show. Maybe that's why Lou picked her. La Serre, it turned out, was her favorite restaurant. She and her family ate there all the time.

The funny thing was, though, that while Sandra sometimes sounded like the worst snob, she really wasn't. She didn't mean to impress you or show off her family's money. She just happened to be rich and she didn't try to hide it. She didn't try to pretend she was an experienced actress either or cover up her jitters. "I don't know what Lou ever saw in me," she'd say to me whenever she messed up. "I don't have a clue about what I'm doing." She learned quickly, though. And she could laugh at her mistakes and was always easy to talk to. I liked her better than any other girl I had ever met.

When we finished the taping, I was sad to say good-bye to her. We promised to call and get together again at the end of summer after she and her family got back from New Mexico. However, deep down I knew that unless the network bought our series we would probably never see one another again.

A THIRTY SHARE

All summer I waited for word about the fate of *The Kid and the Cabbie*. Darlene got so tired of seeing me mope around the house that, at the beginning of July, she shipped me off to Orick to mope around Grandma's house instead. Grandma tried to introduce me to other sixth-graders in town, but it didn't work. The girls in Orick, it seems, hadn't changed since Darlene grew up there. All they wanted to talk about was "Have you ever met Harrison Ford?" or "How do you get to be in television?" Unlike my last visit with Grandma, I was eager to get back home.

One morning, about a week after I returned, Lou showed up unexpectedly at the house. "I was in the neighborhood and thought I'd drop by," he said casually. "How would you and your mom like to go out for lunch?"

"We don't have to go out," Darlene said. "I can make something here."

"No, I insist," Lou said. "I want to take you for a drive."

I looked out the front window and saw a brand-new silver Mercedes convertible parked in our driveway. "They bought the series!" I screamed.

"You got it, kiddo." I was so excited I threw my arms around him.

"They really bought it?" Darlene asked.

"You better believe it. Didn't I tell you we had a winner?" He grabbed Darlene and me each by the hand and led us outside for a spin in his new wheels.

Later that night Darlene took Kelly and me to the Sportsmen's Lodge, our favorite fancy restaurant, for our own private celebration. Kelly seemed less than thrilled by the news, but he came along anyway.

"How much you going to make a week, Meg?" he asked boldly when we were seated.

"I don't know. It's up to Rhonda. She and Darlene make the deals."

"How much you settle on?" Kelly asked Darlene.

"A fair salary."

"C'mon, tell us." Hoping for encouragement, he turned to me. "Don't you want to know how much you're worth on the open market, Meg?"

"I don't care how much I earn," I said. I really didn't.

"Well, I do. I want to know if we're going to be rich or not. How much they paying Meg to be a star?"

"It's none of your business," Darlene said, growing angry.

"Why not?" he argued. "Why shouldn't we know? We're the ones who earn all the money around here. You just spend it." I think Kelly knew immediately that, even if what he had said were true, he had gone too far. Darlene's face went pale in the candlelight, but she didn't say anything. We all just sat there in silence staring at our bread and butter plates. Fortunately, the waiter arrived shortly to take our order and we all continued as if dinner hadn't been ruined.

I knew Kelly hated me for working when no one would hire him, because I had felt the same way about him when we first started out. But what did he want me to do? Turn down the offer? Would that really have made him feel any better?

At the end of August, *The Kid and the Cabbie* went into production. "Welcome to the insanity of a weekly TV series," Lou greeted us on our return.

"It can't be worse than the insanity of the unemployment office," Mort quipped.

I'd never been to the unemployment office, so I couldn't compare it, but *The Kid and the Cabbie* was like nothing else I'd ever done. Each week we turned out another half-hour episode. Monday was for first run-throughs, Tuesday and Wednesday the director blocked the action to set up the camera shots, Thursday we had last rehearsals with the cameras, and Friday we taped (twice) in front of a studio audience. (The best parts of each performance were edited together to create the program that was finally shown on TV.) As we left for home Friday night Lou handed us the script for the next week's show for weekend reading.

Despite the hectic schedule, I loved going to work in the morning. Being a regular on the show was like being adopted into a large family and suddenly acquiring dozens of aunts and uncles. Since Sandra and I were the only kids, everyone seemed to take a special interest in us. People were always dropping by the dressing room we shared to chat. Monica brought us homemade oatmeal cookies, Lou stopped by to tell us jokes, Mort tried to teach us how to read a racing form.

Sometimes all the company was a problem, because in addition to acting, Sandra and I were also supposed to be going to school. Under California law, children from six to sixteen could be on the set for eight hours a day, but we could only work half that time. During the school year three hours of each day had to be spent in classes, and the remaining hour was supposed to be for lunch and breaks.

The studio teacher on our set was Adelaide Fierman, a tall, slender woman in her late twenties who wore exotic clothes and jewelry. Adelaide, we soon learned, had led a very exciting life, had worked on an oil rig in Alaska once, and had traveled around the world on a steamer (which is where she picked up some of her fabulous outfits). What she really wanted to be, she said, was a writer. Teaching was a way to pay the bills until she finished her novel.

Although Adelaide was one of the best teachers I ever had, it was easy to get her off the subject. "That's a pretty skirt," we'd say, "did you get it in Africa?" and she would tell us about one of her adventures. I'm not really sure that we fooled Adelaide, but since she loved to talk she let us get away with it.

Besides our dressing room and classes, the other thing Sandra and I shared was practical jokes. The jokes were usually Sandra's idea, but she always included me in on them. Once she brought in fake nickels and we nailed them to the floor of the set. Then we hid out to watch people try to pick them up. Another time—just before we were to tape a show—Sandra covered her face with grease pencil spots and pretended to have the measles. Lou had a fit before he realized it was a joke. "There's no one easier to con than a con man," Wallace said when we told him about it later.

Besides Sandra, Wallace was the other person on the show whom I considered a good friend, but it took awhile. On the set he was easy to get along with and never seemed to get upset when someone missed a line or cue. Off the set, though, he kept to himself. At lunch he ate alone, in his dressing room, rather than at the studio commissary. If he didn't retreat to his dressing room at breaks, he usually sat shielded by a cloud of cigar smoke and the daily New York Times.

Maybe because Wallace was so mysterious, I was more curious about him than anyone else. Actually, the more I acted with him, the less frightening he seemed. One day during a break, a few weeks after we had been doing the show, I sat down next to him to eat my candy bar. As usual he continued reading his paper.

I got up my courage. "Don't you like people?" I asked.

He put down the front page and considered the question for a bit.

"No, not most people," he finally replied.

"Why not?"

"Experience."

"I guess you must have had some pretty bad ones."

"Enough. You don't turn into a grouch like me overnight."

I wasn't sure if he was teasing or not. "Tony's a grouch," I said, "but underneath he's kind of a softie."

"So you think I might be, too?"

"Maybe."

He took a long puff on his cigar. "Well, don't think I'm going to tell you. You're going to have to make up your mind about that yourself." He turned the page of the newspaper, but he didn't start reading it again.

"What do you think about the show?" I continued. "Do you think it's going to succeed?"

"I'd say it certainly has a chance," he said. "Otherwise I wouldn't have done it. At my age I'm too old to take on any more lost causes. In this business, though, you can never be sure."

"Well, do you think the show's any good?" I persisted.

"Good?" He rolled his cigar between his fingertips. "That's another question. Compared to other television shows or compared to Shakespeare?"

"You don't think much of television, do you?"

He shrugged. "An actor I admire once said that if stage acting is like playing tennis, then movie acting is like Ping-Pong, and TV acting like playing marbles."

"Why do you do it then?"

"Because I'm good at it." He laughed.

After that it was much easier to talk to him. At breaks I'd often take my homework and sit down next to him while he read the *Times*. Sometimes he'd look over my shoulder at my social studies book and comment about what I was reading. Like Adelaide, he knew something about almost everything. He hadn't traveled around the world as she had, but he kept up with what was going on. Often he'd lecture me a little about what was happening in Afghanistan or Poland or El Salvador. Even when the cameras weren't rolling, he liked to deliver speeches.

I didn't care that much about current events, but I really liked to hear him talk about acting. He knew more about it than any director or actor I'd ever met. When I had trouble with a scene, I'd always go to him for help. He rarely offered criticism unless I asked. However, if I did he was always straightforward.

"That stunk, didn't it?" I'd say.

"Like Limburger," he'd answer, or "like the L.A. zoo," or "the '62 Mets." Or he might ask, "What's your goal here? Is this what Carrie really wants, or is it just what she thinks she wants?" Sometimes he'd even suggest a more interesting way to play the scene. "What if you didn't show your anger here? What if you held it back? See how that works for you. If you give them what they're expecting all the time, they begin to take you for granted."

In one of the early episodes there was a running gag that involved a poem, "Why Nobody Pets the Lion at the Zoo," that Carrie had to memorize for school. The poem actually described Carrie's own character and every time she recited it, she messed it up—until the end of the show, when she was finally supposed to get it right. Only I couldn't find a way to do that. Every time I said it, I sounded like a singer hitting a sour note. Finally I went to Wallace.

"I just don't know how to do this," I said. "The poem is dumb and so is the script."

"That may be," he replied, "but your job is to make people

believe the lines are brilliant. A good actress should be able to ask for a glass of water and make her audience cry." He opened the script and found the poem, then he proceeded to read the last few lines in about a dozen different ways.

> "The way to treat a lion right
> Is growl for growl and bite for bite.
>
> True, the Lion is better fit
> For biting than for being bit.
>
> But if you look him in the eye
> You'll find the Lion's rather shy.
>
> He really wants someone to pet him.
> The trouble is: his teeth won't let him.
>
> He has a heart of gold beneath
> But the Lion just can't trust his teeth.

"See," he said when he finished, "there are all sorts of ways to say this poem, but the only real way to do it is the way Carrie would. And that only you and she can discover."

"How did you learn to read like that?" I said, dazzled.

"Practice . . . experience . . . imagination . . . desire. You have the imagination. The desire remains to be seen. If you have that, though, practice and experience only take time."

Some days, especially working together with Wallace, I definitely had the desire to be an actress. Other days I was much less sure that I wanted to spend the rest of my life in front of TV cameras. I would come home completely worn out and with schoolwork to do as well as lines to memorize. I moved from the studio to my house and back again with no detours along the way. The only kids I saw were Sandra, Kelly (who didn't want to see much of me anyway), and the occasional friends of Carrie written into the script that week. Everyone else was older.

Sandra was getting tired of the routine, too. "When I got the part," she said, after almost two months' work, "I thought, gee, Hollywood. I mean, wow, Matt Dillon, Harrison Ford. If they don't drop by the set, for sure I'll see them at the commissary. But where are they? Matt Dillon still doesn't know I'm alive."

"As soon as the show is on the air he will."

"Do you think he watches the tube? Do you have time to any-more?" She was right. If I ever turned it on, I usually fell asleep.

"I miss junior high," she continued her complaints. "I miss my girlfriends. I miss the boys. . . ."

I didn't miss school or any of the boys in my class, but doing the show every week was beginning to get to me, especially since none of the episodes had been broadcast yet. We were scheduled to go on the air as soon as another show was canceled, so it was not until mid-November that *The Kid and the Cabbie* made its debut. By then we had already taped nine shows.

Personally, I had no idea whether anybody would like us. Some-times I thought *The Kid and the Cabbie* was funny, sometimes I didn't. Sometimes I liked my own performances, but often I didn't. When I mentioned the great response of the studio audi-ence, Mort said, pessimistic as usual, "Studio audiences always laugh. That's why they come to the studio, so they can be recorded on a TV laugh track. Then when the show is broadcast they can say to their friends, 'Hear that cackle? That's me.'"

Lou, of course, thought differently. The biggest fan of the show, he found reason for optimism in his own press release. "Do we have a hit or don't we?" he kept saying.

As our opening night approached, the first newspaper reviews began to appear. Most were favorable. "The chemistry between grizzly veteran Wallace Snyder and pixieish newcomer Meg Muldaur could combust into a new hit," said one. Grizzly? Pixieish? "The pairing of a tart-tongued eleven-year-old and a hack-hardened loner is not the most original idea to surface in this year's fall lineup, but as played by roguish Meg Muldaur and churlish Wallace Snyder, it may be among the most promising," said another.

"What's roguish?" I asked Darlene and Kelly.

"Look it up," Darlene suggested.

"Don't bother," Kelly said. "It's only a fancy word for brat."

The night the first show was broadcast, I watched it at home with Darlene and Kelly and Bernie. I had never seen any of the finished shows before, and as usual when I looked at myself on TV I kept a hand near my eyes. Seeing myself on the screen was always a strange experience, like viewing someone trying to imitate you and generally doing an embarrassing job; occasionally, though, the person on the screen would do something that would surprise me and make me wonder how I'd ever thought of that.

Bernie seemed to like what he saw, yapping whenever he noticed me on the screen, but then he barked every time he saw a dog on TV, too. Kelly showed much less emotion.

"So what do you think?" I asked nervously at the first commercial break.

"Wallace is terrific," he said.

"I know he is, but what about me?"

"I liked you better in the corn commercial."

"Oh, Kelly, stop," Darlene chided.

"Okay, you're terrific Meg. You know you are. If you weren't, they wouldn't have picked you. But that kid, Carrie, don't ever bring her home from the studio. She's a real drag." Then he took off for the kitchen and didn't come back until just before the closing credits.

The next morning Lou called us all together at the studio. He announced that according to the overnight Arbitron ratings, *The Kid and the Cabbie* had racked up a very respectable twenty-five share of the audience; in other words, one-quarter of all the TV sets polled in the nation had been tuned to our show. A twenty-six share, Lou explained for Sandra and me, was generally the make-or-break point. If you got less than that, you didn't survive. Lou said it was a very promising start and he knew our audience would only increase. To celebrate he had bought doughnuts for all the cast and crew.

"What a guy!" Mort said. "This afternoon he's probably going to go out and buy himself a Rolls, but he still remembers the little guy."

As the weeks passed Lou's prediction proved accurate. We were not an instantaneous hit, but we had "legs," as he said. Viewers who tuned in to sample us generally tuned in again. By the thirteenth week of the show we were averaging a thirty share, which made us one of the top twenty programs on network television.

There were other signs of our growing popularity: longer lines at the studio to see our tapings, more requests for interviews. One month I was interviewed by *TV Guide*, the *L.A. Times, People, Us*, and *Time* magazine. I said practically the same thing to all of them, but in the end they all wrote different stories. None of them were what I would have written about myself. Reading the articles, seeing myself on the cover of *TV Guide*, it was hard to believe that was really me.

Sometimes I thought of Ryan and wondered if he watched *The Kid and the Cabbie* or read about me. What did he think of his daughter now that she had turned out to be a star? Was he sorry that he'd left us? Or did he read the headlines HOLLYWOOD'S NEWEST BRAT, A KID YOU'LL LOVE TO HATE and feel glad he'd bailed out in time?

Dear Meg,

This is the first time I ever wrote to any TV star, but me and my sister heard about you running away on the news and we couldn't understand it. My sister she got real mad and said you were just a crybaby rich kid and a lot worse things I don't want to write in a letter. But I said no. I figure if you're going to run away from a show that pays you all that money you got to have a pretty good reason.

My sister (she's fourteen) and me (I'm twelve) watch <u>The Kid and the Cabbie</u> every week and like it except for that snooty Sandra Darling. Somebody should change the direction of her nose.

We also saw the pictures in "People" magazine of your birthday party and all the stars who came. The dress you were wearing looked real pretty. I saw a frilly yellow one like it in a fancy dress shop in Detroit and went and tried it on, even though I knew I could never afford to buy it. The saleslady said it looked real good on me, too.

My birthday's a week after yours, but this year I couldn't have a party on account of my dad's still being out of work and his unemployment about run out. Lots of nights now we just have soup beans and potatoes for dinner. But I figure you don't want to hear about that because you got problems of your own. I just want to know what they are.

Your friend,
Marie Danchik

P.S. My sister bet me two weeks of washing dishes that you wouldn't answer this.

Dear Marie,

    I ran away because I was very unhappy with my life and wanted to start over again. It would take a very, very long letter to tell you all the reasons why, but right now I don't feel much like writing anything. I didn't want you to have to do the dishes because of me, though.

    Hoping I'm still your friend,

        Meg Muldaur

CELEBRITY BLUES

Being a celebrity was kind of fun. I liked the attention I got when I went to the market to pick up a quart of milk, and I enjoyed the game of seeing how long it took before someone recognized me. It was satisfying to see people turn their heads when they noticed me or stop and whisper to each other who I was. Wherever I went, people asked me for my autograph—checkers at the supermarket, waiters at restaurants, salesgirls, old ladies on the street. I felt important, powerful. Walking down Ventura Boulevard sometimes I could even stop traffic. But the more people recognized me, the less fun it became.

It was the same way with the show. By the time the first year of production ended in the middle of March, I was happy for a long vacation. Except for two days off at Thanksgiving and two weeks at Christmas, I had worked five days a week for seven months. In that time I had taped twenty-five episodes of the show, given more newspaper and magazine interviews than I could remember, signed enough autographs to develop writer's cramp, and (one of Lou's inspirations) visited at least a half dozen children's wards of hospitals "to spread good cheer" and (incidentally) create publicity for the show.

I hated visiting the hospitals. What did sick and dying children want to see me for? What could I do to make them well? Finally I told Lou I couldn't take any more visits.

"But you make the kids so happy," he said.

"Why?" I asked. It made no sense to me.

"Because you're a star and you take the time to show you care about those less fortunate than you."

After Lou told me that I felt even worse. But the truth was that I was really beginning not to care about any of my fans, sick or well. How can you care about millions of people you don't know?

Every few weeks the network would send over to the studio a sack full of mail I received from viewers. Lou hired a secretary to come in once a week to answer the letters with an autographed picture of me. At first I tried to read all my fan mail, but most of the notes were so sappy and depressing that I quickly stopped. "I want to be just like you." "Your show is my favorite half hour of the week." "Please send me a lock of your beautiful red hair." Why did they think I was so special just because I was on TV? If only they realized that what I wanted most then was to be a more-or-less normal kid! I had played Carrie so much of the time that I was beginning to wonder who was the real me.

Now that I had a break from the show, however, I worried about leading a regular sixth-grade life. After almost a year's absence from school, I was not exactly the most popular member of my class. Working in commercials hadn't endeared me to most of the kids. Would they resent me even more with the show? Think I was even more stuck up? Or would they want to be my friend and share my spotlight?

I reported to Carpenter Elementary as if it were an important audition. But this time no one was there to tell me how to act; there were no lines written for me. I was completely on my own and I didn't know what to expect. When the principal escorted me to Miss Rademacher's sixth-grade class, the only reaction was a ripple of whispers that went up and down the rows of chairs. I took a seat in the back with relief. It was not going to be as bad as I had feared.

But it was no great homecoming either. No one welcomed me back with open arms, not even Miss Rademacher, who spent the morning giving me tests to see how far behind the class I'd fallen. (I think she was disappointed to discover that actually I was a little ahead of them.) I knew most of the kids from my previous years at Carpenter, and they knew me, so it was not as if we had to introduce ourselves all over again. But friendships had already been sealed and cliques were tight. Everyone probably figured I'd be gone in a few months anyway.

The result was that although I chatted with some of the girls between classes, I ate lunch alone. No one joined me either, not even the nerds. On the set I may have been a star, but real life was something else. That night I called Sandra to see how her day had gone. I was sorry to hear it had been terrific. Of course, Sandra was attending a private school where a lot of kids had parents who worked in TV or the movies, so Sandra's being in the business didn't seem strange to them. Only one girl had given her the cold shoulder, and Sandra dismissed her as a "witch." Apparently everyone else in her class was glad to see her back, especially the boys. "It's great," she gushed. "I'm not even too behind in my school work."

Since it was too late for me to switch to a private school, I had to stick it out at Carpenter. As the weeks passed I made a few more friends there, mainly with the black girls who were bussed to school and back, an hour each way, from south central Los Angeles. Like me they were also outsiders. It was the one thing we had in common. Once in a while they would ask me about the show, but none of them were faithful fans. They had all seen it at one time or another, but I think most of them thought it was pretty dumb; it certainly seemed to have little to do with their own lives. They didn't hold my acting in it against me, though. They knew someone was paying me to say Carrie's lines.

I talked to Sandra a lot on the phone at night and we saw each other occasionally on weekends. Away from the show, however, we didn't have quite as much to talk about. Sandra had close friends at school, a life outside of *The Kid and the Cabbie* that she enjoyed. I kept finding, though, that I couldn't escape from Carrie. Even on a break.

One Saturday in April Darlene took Kelly and me to the Sherman Oaks Galleria, a multi-story shopping center in the Valley where a lot of teenagers hung out. While Darlene looked for dresses, Kelly and I went to buy some tapes. A bunch of girls with spiked hair and punk clothing were standing outside the record store smoking and moving to the blasting music. As we approached I saw by their whispering that I was recognized. While Kelly and I looked through the tapes inside the store, I kept glancing at the plate glass entrance. The group was getting larger. Except for the front door, the only other exit was through the back, and I was too embarrassed to ask the store manager if I could use it.

By the time Kelly and I had gone through the checkout line, there were at least a dozen girls outside the store. I followed right behind Kelly and tried to ignore the mob, but it immediately closed in on us. I heard shouts of "Hey, you're Meg Muldaur, aren't you? Say something cold like you do on TV, Meg." And, "Yeah, give us an insult."

It wasn't autographs they wanted. I tried to push through the girls, but they wouldn't give ground. They were so close I could smell their cherry-flavored gum. "I'm sorry, I have to go," I said. I didn't know what else to say. I just wanted to escape.

"C'mon, we're your fans," a tall one, her ear a pincushion of earrings, said challengingly.

"Yeah, you can't cut your fans," someone else sneered.

Then suddenly one of them reached over Kelly and touched my cheek with her sticky fingers. I felt myself curl up inside. "I touched her. I touched Meg Muldaur," she said crazily.

I pushed Kelly forward like a blocking back but it didn't work.

Suddenly they were all reaching for me, pawing at my face, my hair, tearing at the buttons of my jacket. I think Kelly was as terrified as I. With a tremendous lunge he finally broke through the circle and I followed on his heels. We didn't stop running until we reached the car.

I sat inside, unable to stop shaking, wanting desperately to rush home and shower, to wash any trace of those dirty, gummy fingers from my skin.

"So that's what it's like to be a star," Kelly said softly. "God, I'm glad I gave up acting."

SECOND YEAR SLIDE

At the beginning of August we started shooting the second season of *The Kid and the Cabbie*. The first day was like a big family reunion with everyone on the set kissing and hugging each other. After Wallace squeezed me, he stepped back, removed the cigar from his mouth, and gave me a thorough examination.

"You've grown," he concluded.

"It's what happens to kids," I said, "especially twelve-year-olds." It was not only that I had grown an inch and a half during our five-month break, but I was beginning to fill out in other places as well. "Dreaded puberty," to use Kelly's phrase, was finally catching up with me.

"I hope Lou and his writers have noticed," he said.

"It's hard to hide."

"That's true." He smiled.

I suddenly felt self-conscious. "This won't ruin things, will it?" I asked.

"Elizabeth Taylor survived puberty. No reason why you shouldn't, too. Besides change is good for a series, generates new plots."

Lou seemed much less confident. "God, you've sprouted," he exclaimed. The way he said it made it sound like a crime.

"I'll stop drinking milk," I said.

"What's done is done." He sighed.

"Carrie couldn't stay the same forever," I tried to console him.

"Why not? This is television, Meg, not real life."

Lou's disappointment was clear. By growing, somehow, I had personally let him down. I knew they could not fire me from the series—Rhonda had just renegotiated my contract for the year— but the change in my physical appearance obviously concerned Lou. Of course, he had other problems as well. Besides my sudden growth spurt, the network had switched our time slot from Wednesday to Monday night in order to strengthen its Monday schedule. The network felt our audience would be faithful enough to follow us, but Lou feared the shift. He didn't want to do anything to tamper with success. He wanted to keep Carrie the same age, the same size, on Wednesday nights at eight-thirty forever. Even in television, it couldn't be done.

First of all, the two writers who had written most of our first season's shows went to work for another program. Lou found new writers, but the scripts were not as good. Then there was a lot of grumbling among the cast. Mort wanted more lines and the rumor was that he wanted more money, too. Monica Hale didn't like the show's hairdresser. Sandra did not get along with a new director. Even Adelaide complained that Lou was working Sandra and me more than the legal limit of four hours a day.

Because of all these reasons—or maybe others—something began to go wrong. "Sophomore jinx," suggested Mort. "The new writers," Wallace contended. "They don't understand the show's dynamics yet." "No cute boys," was Sandra's explanation. But I wondered if Lou's first instincts weren't right—if I was growing too old to play the Carrie he had created.

Whatever the cause, from the first episode of the new year, the ratings began to slip. Morale on the set began to fall, too. There was no longer the same energy or enthusiasm there had been our first season. Everyone seemed tight, as if they were all looking for someone else to blame for the falling ratings. With everyone so critical you dreaded to make any mistake. Once the director Sandra didn't like yelled so much at her for missing a cue during rehearsal that she fled the set in tears. "My father was right about TV," she cried later in our dressing room.

The more the ratings dropped, the more rumors we heard that the show was going to be canceled or not renewed for the next year. Lou denied them all. "We're going to turn this around," he kept saying. "It's just this new time slot. That's the only thing that's killing us." Nevertheless he fired the hairdresser, two of his new writers, and the director who had made Sandra cry. None of it made any difference in the numbers. In order for the show to survive, we all knew there had to be more drastic changes.

Only Wallace seemed to rise above it all. "Last year we were all celebrities, this year we're washouts. Were we really that much better before?" he asked. "Never believe your press clippings. Distrust them most when they are raves. Remember what Stanislavsky said, 'Learn to love the art in you, not the you in art.'"

I didn't know who Stanislavsky was and I didn't understand his advice. "All I want to know is what happens if the show is canceled," I said impatiently.

"Then we'll all find other work. You're not expecting to go on playing Carrie until you're fifty, are you?"

I didn't know what I expected anymore. All I knew was that it was harder and harder to go to Burbank every day.

By the day we taped the final show of the season I was thoroughly beat, drained, and discouraged. If I could get through that March afternoon, though, I knew I might never have to utter another of Carrie's putdowns again. Between tapings, Wallace invited me into his dressing room. "I have the feeling that you've stopped liking Carrie," he said gently. I hadn't thought about it before, but I knew that he was right. "I have been playing her pretty mean, haven't I?" I admitted.

"What is it that makes you so angry with her?" "She seems so trapped," I blurted out, "in her life, the show. Nobody will let her be herself."

"Use that feeling," he said sternly. "Use it to try to understand Carrie. Don't hold it against her."

"It's too late now. The series won't be renewed."

"It's not too late for this afternoon's taping."

I thought about what he said and for at least a half hour that afternoon was able to forgive Carrie. Her situation was, after all, not so different from my own.

I don't know if anyone else noticed the difference in my performance, but certainly Wallace did. For his sake I was glad to finish the season on a positive note.

"Will we ever see each other again?" I asked after what I was sure was our last episode.

He put his arm around me. "My dear," he said, "don't you know me by now? Do you think I'd let the tastes of a few million viewers come between us?"

Six weeks later, to my surprise, the network decided to renew *The Kid and the Cabbie* for another year. Lou took Darlene and me to lunch to celebrate. This time it was not at La Serre.

"I have some good news and some bad news," Lou told us over corned beef sandwiches at the local deli. "The good news you already know. The show has been renewed and so have you. The bad news is that several of your friends are going to be leaving us."

"Not Wallace?" I said in alarm.

"No, not Wallace, but just about everybody else."

"Everybody?" I said, stunned.

"Sandra, Mort, Monica," he ticked them off. "You and Wallace are moving to a new neighborhood next year. Network research has shown we're not appealing to a wide enough audience. We need to attract more minority viewers, more middle-aged women, more teenagers. We're looking for a black actor to be Wallace's best friend and we're going to find a love interest for Wallace. Romance is supposed to be the key to attracting 'female viewers in their middle years.'" He shrugged as if he had no choice.

"I agreed to all that," he went on, "because that's what the network wanted, but between you and me, those changes are just cosmetic. They're not what's going to save this show."

"What is?" I asked glumly.

"You are."

"Me?"

"You." He nodded.

Darlene nodded in agreement.

"I know this is going to cost me money when I sit down with Rhonda, but I told your mom this over the phone, and I'm telling you truthfully now—you're the real reason the network decided to gamble on another season. You're the key to pulling in the teenage audience, and that's what's going to make or break the show next fall.

"We made a mistake last season," he admitted. "We should have taken more advantage of your development. This year we're going to turn it into our biggest asset. You're the person who's going to turn us around, Meg." I tried to hide my panic by searching in my jeans pockets for a tissue, but I couldn't find any. Why me? I thought. Why not Sandra?

Lou reached over and took my hand. "I believe in you, kid," he said. "Your mom believes in you. The network believes in you. We all know you can do it. This is your breakthrough year, thirteen, the year you start dating and wearing trendy dresses. Sex and clothes, that's what teenagers care about," he said confidently.

I didn't know if those were his opinions or the research department's, but if they were really true, I knew he had fired the wrong actress. Sandra was the one who liked boys and dresses. She should have stayed, not me. I knew, though, there was no use in arguing with him. The network had already made its decision.

I put off calling Sandra for as long as I could, but finally around ten that night I got up my courage. We had been with each other every weekday for half of two full years now and although we sometimes got on each other's nerves, she was still the closest friend I had.

"You don't hate me, do you?" I asked.

"Oh, Meg, don't be stupid. You're not the one who fired me."

"Lou shouldn't have done it."

"It wasn't Lou, it was the network," she defended him. "Anyway I was kind of expecting it. I didn't think the show was going to be renewed." She sounded almost sorry that it had been or maybe that was just the way I was feeling myself.

"You'll get other parts," I tried to cheer her up. "Probably a lot better ones."

"I don't know if I want any more parts. I'm really not that good, you know."

"Sure you are," I lied a little bit.

"No, not like you. You're the real actress. Besides it wasn't as fun as I thought it would be. Matt Dillon was never going to come by anyway. I think he's crossed Burbank off his list for good."

"Well, maybe he's looking for a leading lady for his next film," I teased, but Sandra wasn't in the mood for joking.

"I don't care about Matt Dillon anymore, and I don't care about the show. I think I'll be a lawyer when I grow up."

"We'll still be friends, won't we?" I asked.

"You kidding?" Still, when I hung up I felt as if we'd just said good-bye for good.

LOU THROWS A PARTY

For my thirteenth birthday in June, Lou decided to throw a party. "Just a little celebration," he told me on the phone, "to announce to the world that you've become a teen . . . and that *The Kid and the Cabbie* is still alive."

"Do we really need a party to do that?" I asked.

"I thought you'd love the idea." He sounded disappointed. "Everybody loves a good party, especially the press. They love the free food, the booze, the photo opportunities. We'll get terrific coverage."

"Do I have to come?" I grumbled.

"A joke," he laughed. "That was a joke, I hope."

I didn't say anything.

"Hey, thirteen's the magic age." He tried to sell me on his idea. "It's the end of childhood, the beginning of maturity—a turning point. It *demands* a celebration."

I could tell that there was no way to talk him out of it. "How big a party are you thinking about?"

"Oh, just a few hundred people . . . ."

I hung up feeling sick. The party wasn't for me; it was to promote the show. I could understand why Lou wanted to publicize our survival, but I didn't feel much like celebrating Sandra's firing.

I tried to explain to Darlene, but she stuck up for Lou. "I know you're upset about Sandra," she said, "and I am, too. But that's part of the business. You know that. The show goes on, no matter what happens to the people in it. Besides, it's not as if you'll never see Sandra again."

It was not just Lou's dropping Sandra from the series, though, that made me want to skip the party. The more I thought about next season, the more I dreaded returning to it. Darlene liked the idea of the new Carrie, but I didn't know the first thing about boys. The only one my age I'd ever spent much time with was Kelly, and since I'd started playing Carrie, even he didn't want much to do with me.

Going to the same school that year, Reed Junior High, didn't help matters with Kelly either. When Darlene dropped us off at school in the morning, he would dash off as if I had some kind of communicable disease, and most days I didn't see him again till dinner. I had thought changing schools would be a chance to meet new people. However, by the time I joined my class in March, everybody already knew who I was—or thought they did—and had made up their minds about me. It was Carpenter all over again.

"You know you'll never make friends if you don't make any effort," Kelly lectured me one of the rare afternoons we rode the bus home together.

"People don't give *me* a chance," I said angrily.

"Because you act like the Queen of England or something."

"I do not," I protested. "That's not true." I felt my eyes smarting. "Nobody wants to have anything to do with me. Not even you. You run away as if I were contaminated."

"Nobody helped me make friends when I started at Reed," he said flatly. "You've got to do it on your own."

Maybe Kelly was right, but that spring I felt that nobody was on my side. Sandra didn't call much, Wallace was away, and Darlene thought that a few months' rest from the show was all I needed to make me eager to return. There was no one I could really talk to. I thought about Ryan again and remembered that day at the beach when my kite had crashed in the ocean. But it seemed a silly thing to even think about. Ryan had been gone for years and I no longer cried over things like kites except for the times I was asked to in a script.

Darlene was convinced Lou's party would cheer me up. Not only would it be a great boost for the show, but it would also be a good way for me to make new friends. "You can invite as many kids as you want," she said. "There'll be plenty of room." Lou had rented a banquet room at the Beverly Wilshire Hotel. There was enough space for my entire junior high class. The problem was there was no one at Reed I wanted to invite. I thought of asking some of my old friends from Carpenter, but I'd lost touch with most of them. The only real friend I had was Sandra, and I wasn't sure if she would want to come. I called her anyway.

"I'll have to talk to my parents," she said vaguely. "We may be away that weekend."

I knew she was trying to find an excuse that wouldn't hurt my feelings, and I understood the reasons.

"You don't have to come," I said. "The party's really for Lou. I'd like to skip it myself."

"Why don't you?" she asked.

It was a logical question, but I didn't have quite enough nerve. Besides, it was my birthday celebration, even if I didn't have any friends to invite.

Lou was not pleased by my guest list. "You can't have a thirteen-year-old birthday party with just adults," he said.

"Why not?"

"Because it doesn't look right."

"Why?"

"Because thirteen-year-olds should have friends their own age," he said.

"But I don't," I replied.

"You're a wonderful kid, Meg, but you've got to give people a chance to know you. Break the ice, invite them to the party."

I shook my head. "I'm not inviting people who don't like me," I said as firmly as I could.

"We're not asking you to invite anybody you hate, Meg," he said, patiently. "Besides, there are other things involved in this. You're a star of a major television series and you have responsibilities to that series . . . to the network who pays for it . . . to the *millions* of viewers who are your fans. I got *People* magazine coming to this party, *Time, Super Teen. Super Teen*'s not sending a photographer to take *my* picture. The photographer's coming to snap *you*, you and your friends. This is for the teen audience we have to reach this year if the show is going to survive. Is that too much to ask?"

"You want teenagers there, you invite them. It's your party, not mine," I said, ending the discussion.

When I entered the ballroom at the Beverly Wilshire, things were exactly as I had feared. Although I was the guest of honor, there weren't many faces that I recognized—and most of those I did I only knew from watching TV. Lou wanted kids so he had rounded up a couple of dozen himself. I don't know where he found them—on the streets of Westwood or from some casting agency—but I didn't know a single one. No one seemed to notice, though. BIRTHDAY BASH FOR THE BRAT, *Variety* headlined its story about the occasion. "Dozens of Hollywood celebs turned up at the Beverly Wilshire Saturday to fete TV's reigning hoyden. . . ."

If you saw the pictures in *People* you know that the network didn't spare any expenses. There were not one, but two bands, one new wave, the other rockabilly. The waiters poured champagne as if it were Kool-Aid, and there was so much food on the buffet tables that I lost my appetite looking at them. The cake was the largest I had ever seen. Decorated to look like a wide-screen TV set, it framed a gigantic marzipan portrait of me.

There was a picture of me in *People* cutting the cake in my lemon chiffon party dress that Darlene had specially picked out for me and that was a bit too tight. She is standing on one side of me and Lou on the other, both looking quite pleased with themselves. And I am smiling at the photographer as if I am the happiest thirteen-year-old in the world.

But it is all a pose, an act, phonier than any commercial I ever did. I was smiling so much that my mouth was beginning to feel as tight as my dress, and my head was starting to spin from the glass of champagne I'd sneaked and all the noise of the party.

Then I went searching the ballroom for someone safe, someone I didn't have to smile at or be nice to. Finally, I spotted Kelly, off in the corner talking to the prettiest of Lou's rent-a-kids. He really had learned to make friends, and I hated him for it.

Turning, I saw Lou steering yet another stranger toward me from across the room. The rock band blared behind me, the ballroom began to whirl, and suddenly my stomach began to churn.

I bolted from the party and escaped into the ladies' room. There was no one there but the white-uniformed attendant, a tiny black woman with close-cropped frizzy gray hair, who was sitting in a chair reading *True Romance* magazine.

I ran some water in a sink to wash my face and compose myself. The attendant put down her magazine and brought over a towel. She held it patiently as she watched me in the mirror.

"That's a pretty dress," she said. "I always like a lemon color dress."

I didn't say anything.

She handed me the towel. "It sounds like a nice party," she went on.

"It isn't," I muttered, drying my face. "It's a terrible party."

She didn't seem particularly surprised to hear it.

"They give a lot of terrible parties at this hotel," she said. "This one for some TV star I guess."

I realized then that she didn't know who I was. For the first time that afternoon I didn't have to be careful about what I said.

"I bet a lot of people come in here to hide out from the parties, don't they?" I asked.

"Oh, honey, you don't know how many. The stories I could tell you. . . ." She seemed happy that I had asked. "I been working here fifteen years now and I seen all kinds of things," she continued. "Some days I come to work thinking about my troubles and feeling sorry for myself and I sit in that chair and listen to the ladies talk about their miseries and I go home feeling so much better. Rich ladies, with diamonds and sequined gowns, pretty as you see in magazines, and they come in here with tears running down their cheeks, wishing they could change their lives. I listen to their troubles and think I wouldn't trade my uniform for their fancy dresses any day. Better to be poor than some of those women. You're just a child, honey, so you wouldn't know. . . ."

She went on, but I stopped listening. It was so simple I wondered why I had never thought of it before. There was no reason I couldn't change my life if I wanted. Maybe it was hard for the rich ladies to give up their sequined gowns, but it would be easy for me to give up Hollywood. All I had to do was run away and start over again where no one knew me.

"Thanks," I said to the attendant, handing her back the damp towel. "You don't know how glad I am that I came in here."

Dear Margaret Muldaur,

You probably don't remember me, but a long time ago I was in your class at Hollywood Dance. I got the chicken pox the day before the recital and you borrowed my costume. My mom says that's how you got discovered.

The Kid and the Cabbie is not my favorite show on TV, although I guess you're OK in it. I'd like to have the chance to act on TV too, but I don't have an agent.

My mom says that if I hadn't got sick, maybe I would have been discovered instead of you. Since you never paid us for the costume you used, she says maybe you could introduce me to your agent.

Sincerely,
Mary Lou Mizer

LEAVING HOME

Having made up my mind to split, the next step was to decide where to go. There was no point in taking off unless I was going to end up some place better. I knew kids ran away from home all the time. (In fact, an article I read in the *L.A. Times* said about a million and a quarter of them run away every year in this country.) Most of them, though, wind up panhandling in New York or San Francisco or Hollywood. I had seen the runaways huddling in the doorways or sleeping in the phone booths on Hollywood Boulevard. That wasn't my idea of a better life. What I wanted was to go somewhere nobody knew me, a quiet, pretty town someplace with normal people where I could be just like any other school kid. I considered a number of cities, but it was hard to make up my mind from pictures in magazines and the encyclopedia. Finally I decided on Portland, Oregon.

I chose Portland for several reasons. First, it looked pretty, a little like Orick with tall fir trees and heavy mist. Then the magazines said it was an "outdoor city," and all the kids they showed were wearing shorts or jeans, so I liked that. But most of all, I guess, I picked it because Ryan still lived there. Since I hadn't seen him in eight years, I had no idea if I'd want to live with him, or if he'd even want to take me in, but I knew he'd never tell Darlene where I was hiding or force me to go back to L.A.

Once I had made up my mind about Portland, I made up a list of all the things I had to do to get ready. I won't bore you with all the details, but it took me several weeks to cross out everything on the list. I tried to do it all as casually as possible to avoid calling any attention to myself. Instead of withdrawing the money from my savings account all at once, for example, I took it a little bit at a time, until finally I had $2,000. I even left fifty dollars in my account to keep it open so no one would ask any sticky questions.

Now I know $2,000 is not a lot of money to start a new life, but the truth is that's all the money I could get my hands on. The rest was tied up in trusts or other accounts that required Darlene's or our lawyer's signature. From the thousands of dollars I'd made, the only amount I controlled completely was the $2,050 in my savings account, which I'd slowly built from my twenty-five dollar a week allowance. I hoped it would be enough.

I had no difficulty withdrawing my money or reserving a one-way ticket to Portland in a fictitious name. I was nervous carrying all that cash around with me, so I hid most of it under the heel pad in my sneakers. What worried me more, though, was my looks. How was I ever going to run away in secret when practically every place I went people recognized my burnt orange hair and face full of freckles? I knew I needed a really good disguise, but I had to wait until the last moment to test it.

I made my plane reservation for Saturday morning, because on Saturdays Darlene and Kelly usually slept late. The night before I set my alarm for five minutes past one. When it went off, Darlene and Kelly were both sound asleep. I locked myself in the bathroom with a bottle of hair coloring and scissors, and ninety minutes later I flushed the last lock of red hair down the toilet. The face that stared back at me in the mirror was ghastly—a punk-rocker with chicken pox—but I felt an unexpected sense of elation. The adorable, pixieish Margaret O'Brien Muldaur was no more. Mary Ann Spring had just been born.

After dabbing on heavy makeup to hide my freckles, I returned to my bedroom, and quietly packed the Louis Vuitton suitcase that a network bigwig had given me for my birthday. If he only knew what I was using it for!

I wasn't exactly sure what to take along, but I threw in mostly jeans and shorts and T-shirts. The magazines I'd read said it rained a lot in Portland, so I made sure to bring my yellow rain slicker. To be safe, I decided I'd better take one dress and a pair of good shoes as well. I couldn't remember Ryan ever wearing a suit, but maybe he had changed.

When I'd finished packing, there were still a lot of clothes hanging in my closet and a lot of junk scattered about the room— stuffed animals on my dresser, kites hanging on the walls, records and scripts and bumper stickers. All I ended up taking was a scruffy white stuffed kitten with one glass eye that Kelly had given me for my seventh birthday, my favorite dragon kite, my Sony Walkman and a few tapes, and a picture of me and Wallace Snyder taken on the set in front of his taxi. Wallace had the picture framed for me and inscribed it, "To the only actress who has ever upstaged me." I left the rest.

When I finally shut the suitcase, it was four-thirty in the morning, which left me two hours until the cab I had ordered would arrive. That gave me plenty of time to strip the sheets, straighten up my room, and compose my good-bye letter.

It turned out that I needed all one hundred and twenty minutes, for when I sat down at my desk, I had difficulty deciding what to write. The more I thought about it, though, the more I was sure that no matter what I said Darlene wouldn't understand anyway. I didn't know about Kelly. Several times I'd thought about telling him my plans, but I was afraid he might try to talk me out of them, or else want to come with me himself. Maybe once I got settled I could send for him.

I sat there, watching the palm tree outside my window slowly turn from black to gray, worrying over what I should write. I finally picked up my pen and scrawled:

Dear Darlene and Kelly and Bernie,

I've thought about this a long time and I've decided that the best way to solve my problems is to leave home and start over again.

I know I'll miss all of you, but I'll write when I get settled and maybe we can all see each other again sometime.

Kelly, you can have anything you want in my room, but don't bother looking for my Walkman because I took it with me.

Darlene, do whatever you want with my clothes. Maybe you can sell the dresses. Most of them are as good as new.

Bernie can have all my socks and stuffed animals to chew. That should last him a few weeks.

I hope you all won't be too mad at me for this.

Love, Meg

After I finished the note, I got dressed, tying a handkerchief-sized scarf around my head to try to conceal the fright wig I'd made of my hair. Then I carefully carried my suitcase and my shoes to the front door. I didn't really need to worry about waking Darlene and Kelly, though, for both of them are the type who sleep through earthquakes. My biggest fear was Bernie, but I had a giant dog biscuit ready to shove in his mouth when he came bounding up to see me.

I left my note on the dining-room table along with my keys. In the carpeted room, I put on my shoes and sunglasses, picked up my suitcase, and walked out of the house.

To be extra safe I had given the taxi the address of the house at the corner instead of my own, so I had to lug my bag for another half block. Luckily, there was no one on the street. The only person I encountered was a woolly-haired neighbor who stepped outside to fetch his morning paper from the rose bushes. In his torn Mickey Mouse T-shirt and his red Jockey underpants, however, he looked as embarrassed to see me as I did to discover him, and he quickly ducked inside. I leaned up against a palm and tried to look as inconspicuous as I could.

Fortunately the Valley cab arrived a little early. "You the Spring party?" the young driver asked as he pulled up to the curb.

"That's me, Mary Ann Spring." I tried out my new alias.

The driver got out of the car and looked me over as if something about my appearance bothered him. He didn't look so respectable himself. There were crumbs among the orchids of his red Hawaiian sport shirt and he badly needed a shave.

"You all alone?" he asked.

"Just me."

He opened the trunk and tossed in my suitcase. I got in the backseat of the taxi and we started off for the Burbank airport. As we drove, he kept glancing back at me in his rearview mirror, studying me as he polished off a sugar doughnut from a box on the seat next to him.

Finally, at a traffic light, he turned and boldly stared at me. "I got to say it," he said, as if he were doing something noble. "The disguise you're wearing is one of the worst I've ever seen."

"I don't know what you're talking about," I said weakly.

"C'mon," he countered. "I watch your show all the time. Even with the wig, I know you're Meg Muldaur."

"That's not a wig." I pulled a clump of my hair to prove it. "I'm afraid you've made a mistake."

"Whatever you say." He shrugged and drove a few more blocks in silence. The meter loudly ticked off the fare.

"Want a doughnut?" He extended the box in what I took to be a peace gesture.

I declined the offer.

He took another one himself. "Look, Meg," he tried again.

"Mary Ann," I corrected. "The name is Mary Ann Spring." Even as I said it, I wondered why I had chosen such a turkey of a name.

"Okay, if you don't want to admit it, that's cool. I don't want to pry. I mean it's none of my business who your hairdresser is, right? Or why you're covering up your pretty freckles with all that goop. . . ."

"It *is* none of your business," I insisted.

"Amazing how much like her you sound." He gave me a quick, powdered-sugar-flecked smile over his shoulder.

I didn't reply. One thing I couldn't disguise was my voice.

My silence did not discourage him. "It so happens," he continued, "that I'm a real fan of your show. It's not just that I drive a hack. I also happen to be a student of the media, a graduate of UCLA film school and"—he paused dramatically—"an aspiring screenwriter myself." He glanced at me in the rearview mirror to check my reaction.

I stared out the side window. He went on anyway.

"As a faithful follower of your show, I also happen to be aware of its drop in ratings this year. Now I don't know if this early morning trip to the airport has anything to do with those problems . . ."

"I *really* don't want to talk about it," I said as emphatically as I could.

He finally got the message. "I hear you," he said, sounding a little hurt. "I do." He consoled himself with another doughnut. "All I was trying to say is that if you want to talk you have a sympathetic ear."

I kept my eyes on the side window. The driver said nothing more until we approached the airport. Then he made up for lost time.

"I want you to know that it was a real privilege to drive you today. When I said before that I followed your show these last two years, I should have added that it's about the only TV program that I do watch regularly. I'm not telling you this to con you, or to wangle a bigger tip, but because it's true. Generally, I hate TV. Who doesn't? So why do I want to write for it? you ask. A fair question. Well, I know I can do better. Take your show, for instance. To be perfectly frank, this year the scripts have been stinko. Your writers have forgotten what the show is all about. You and Wallace, that's the key. The little orphan Annie appeal, Jackie Coogan and the champ, the foundling trying to find someone to love her who ends up saving all the adults. That's the heart of it. But this year you lost it. If you don't mind my saying so, Carrie was getting to be a real pain in the butt, the kind of kid you wanted to lock up in a juvenile detention home. I've given a lot of thought to this. . . ."

Luckily, we pulled up in front of the terminal. "I know you're not responsible for the scripts, of course," he quickly concluded, then paused and turned around to face me, "and I hope your ratings problems aren't the reason you're running away, because the show definitely can be saved. . . ."

"I told you before," I snapped. "You've made a mistake. I'm not the person you think I am."

I could see the disappointment in his face. He turned and shut off the meter. The fare was $11.40.

He got out of the car and removed my suitcase from the trunk. I pulled out fifteen dollars from my wallet and handed it to him.

"For Meg Muldaur, no charge." He handed the money back.

"The name is Mary Ann Spring," I declared firmly, and shoved the money back into his hand. "Keep the change," I added.

He hesitated but took it. I grabbed my bag from him and started inside.

"Wait," he insisted. He fumbled through his wallet and pulled out a smudged and faded business card, as worn as an old dollar bill. "If you're ever looking for a writer who can turn your show around, give me a call." He pressed the card into my hand. "Good luck . . . Meg." He smiled and headed toward his cab.

When I glanced at the wrinkled card, I saw he had also returned my money. Maybe I should have been grateful, but I wasn't. I didn't want any favors from anyone, not for being a TV star.

PORTLAND

After that cab ride I was prepared for the worst, but once inside the crowded terminal everything went smoothly. The airplane ticket I had reserved in the name of M. Spring was waiting for me and no one asked me to prove that I was the same person. I didn't want to take the chance of anyone recognizing me, though, so I spent most of the time before take-off in a corner hiding behind a copy of *Life* magazine.

Once aboard the plane I began to relax a little bit. Even with my sunglasses, no one seemed to give me a second glance. I had a window seat toward the rear of the plane next to a businessman type with a scuffed leather briefcase. He smiled absently at me as I took my seat, but he was too occupied with his papers to start up any conversation.

I didn't mind, though, because I was so tired that as soon as I had my juice and sweet roll, I fell asleep and didn't awaken until the plane began its approach to Portland. When I saw the snow-covered mountains in the distance, the sparkling river and the lush, tree-covered hills, I knew I had made the right decision.

There was no one at the airport waiting to welcome me to my new life, but there were no policemen either waiting to return me to L.A. I felt like doing cartwheels as I headed for the baggage area. I had pulled it off. I had escaped.

As I waited for my suitcase, I found a phone booth and looked up Ryan's number. There were only a half dozen Muldaurs listed and only one Ryan. It had to be my father. I hesitated a few minutes before I dialed his number, trying to decide on the best opening line. "Hey, Dad, this is Meg," or "This is your daughter, Margaret." I finally chose the second because it seemed more grown up to me.

I put a quarter in the telephone and dialed the number. The pounding of my heart sounded louder than the ringing on the other end of the line. A woman answered. A woman! Had I dialed the wrong number? "Hello . . . hello," she repeated.

"Is . . . is Ryan Muldaur there?" I finally managed to stammer.

"I'm sorry. I can barely hear you," she said. "This is a terrible connection. Please dial again." She hung up.

I sat there in the booth trying to work up my courage to call again, but the lines I had rehearsed had been for the wrong scene. I had not been prepared for a woman to answer the phone. All the times I had imagined this conversation I had expected to speak to Ryan. Now I needed time to think of a new opening, so I decided to head into Portland and look around.

The ride in on the airport bus was uneventful. The day was sunny, the air clear. The city looked as pretty as the pictures I had seen. From the bus window I caught glimpses of children and dogs chasing each other through the sprinklers on the green lawns of pine-shaded homes. I wondered if Ryan lived in any of those places. Of course if I had seen him washing his car or trimming the shrubs, I wasn't sure I would have known him.

The bus stopped at several downtown hotels. I didn't want to wander around town with my suitcase, and I worried about reaching Ryan right away. The safest thing to do, it seemed, was to check into a hotel for the night. I picked the Benson Hotel because the elderly couple in matching straw hats in the seat across from me got off there. Although they both had gray hair, they acted like newlyweds, holding hands all the way from the airport. They looked like the kind of people who wouldn't stay just any place.

The Benson turned out to be what Darlene would call "refined": red carpet, polished brass, uniformed bellmen. The doorman ushered me in as if I were a visiting dignitary. At first I thought he had recognized me, then I realized it was probably just my fancy suitcase that earned me such respect.

I had never checked into a hotel by myself before, so I lagged behind the straw-hatted couple watching to see what they did. When they had registered, I stepped up to the desk and asked for a single room.

"Do you have a reservation?" the clerk asked.

"I'm sorry I don't."

"I don't know if we have anything available."

"Oh, I *so* hope you can find a place," I said, doing my best to appear desperate. I guess I was pretty convincing because the clerk started looking through his file.

"Well, maybe I can find something," he said. "You traveling alone?"

"My aunt will be joining me tomorrow. She's coming from Fairbanks, Alaska, but she missed her plane this morning." I went on at length about my world-traveling aunt and how she said "in Portland the Benson is the only place to stay." I was afraid I was laying it on a little thick. Perhaps, though, in refined hotels they were not used to people lying, or maybe the clerk just wanted to get rid of me. In any case, he finally managed to locate a room. It was expensive enough, eighty-five dollars, that I almost regretted my elaborate story, but I didn't feel much like wandering around the city looking for another place to stay.

I registered in my new name, Mary Ann Spring, and paid in cash right away.

"I trust we will live up to your aunt's recommendation," the clerk said, summoning a bellman.

The bellman was a sour, red-faced, older man who was not

much taller than I was. I thought he kept looking at me oddly. "Haven't I seen you before, miss?" he finally asked.

"Whenever I'm passing through Portland I stay here," I said as if I spent half of my life staying at hotels. To make sure he didn't pry anymore, I tipped him five dollars.

Alone in my room, I turned on the TV and flopped on the queen-size bed. I had successfully run away from home and registered at a ritzy hotel. Now what was I going to do? I didn't have to spend a long time thinking about the answer. Having been up most of the previous night, I promptly fell asleep.

When I awoke it was late in the afternoon and an old movie of Wallace's was running on TV. I'd seen it before, but I watched it anyway. Wallace played a surly, hard-boiled newspaper editor, whom everybody in the film hated. "If you're playing a villain, always look for his good points," Wallace once told me. "If you're playing a hero, always look for his flaws." Although the editor treated everybody miserably, Wallace still made you feel sorry that nobody liked him. There was one scene in which he was drinking alone in his office late at night and calling up people and bawling them out on the phone. It almost made me cry. Here I wasn't even gone a day and already I missed Wallace. I wondered if I'd ever see him again.

I was hungry when the movie was over, so I walked outside looking for a restaurant where I could get a good hamburger. Nobody on the streets of downtown Portland seemed to take any notice of me or my disguise.

Finally I found a restaurant that looked popular and I went in and ordered a strawberry milk shake, hamburger, and fries. While I ate my dinner, I studied the people in the restaurant, trying to imagine what their lives were like. There were college student types who may have been on dates, families out for a Saturday night dinner and perhaps a movie, and a table of girls my age who kept eyeing a nearby table of boys. I was about the only person sitting by myself.

The sun was setting in a rose-colored sky as I walked back to the

Benson. The elderly couple emerged from the hotel, without their straw hats, but still arm in arm. The woman smiled at me as I passed.

Back in my room I rehearsed the lines I had prepared for calling Ryan. After panicking on my first attempt I was more nervous than ever, but finally I took Wallace's advice for curing stage fright— walk onstage—and I dialed the number.

This time a man answered.

"Ryan Muldaur?" I asked, trying not to swallow my voice.

"Speaking."

"This is your daughter, Margaret."

"Meg?" he gulped.

"I'm here in Portland."

Several seconds passed before he responded.

"Is your mother with you?"

"No, I'm alone." I couldn't tell whether that was the right answer or not, so I went on, "I'm at the Benson Hotel. I'm just passing through," I added for reassurance.

"At the Benson," he repeated, as if it were not the place he would have picked himself.

"I'd like to see you," I said.

There was another long pause. I was sure then he'd say no.

"How about tomorrow morning?" he finally suggested. "Are you doing anything then?"

"No, I'm free tomorrow."

"I'll pick you up then at the hotel, about nine."

"Fine, I'll wait for you in the lobby."

"I guess I shouldn't have any trouble recognizing you. I've seen you on TV."

"Well, I've cut my hair since then, and it's a little darker."

"I figure I'll still recognize you."

"Well, I'll see you tomorrow then."

"Yeah, at nine. Don't have breakfast."

"I won't."

There was another awkward pause.

"Okay then," he said and hung up.

I lay on the bed and replayed the phone call in my mind, but no matter how I changed my lines, I couldn't seem to alter Ryan's cool replies.

A VISIT TO THE ZOO

I awoke at six-thirty, showered, washed and dried my hair, and tried to decide how to dress for the occasion. What do you wear to meet a father you haven't seen in eight years? I put on a pair of clean jeans and a T-shirt, but somehow they didn't seem right, so I tried the dress I'd brought—a simple, dignified, turquoise-blue, V-necked cotton dress from Saks. That looked better to me, more grown-up. The only jewelry I had with me were a gold necklace and matching earrings that Darlene had given me for my birthday. This reunion with Ryan seemed important enough to wear them, though. I even added a few touches of blush and a little claret lip gloss. Examining myself in the mirror I thought that Darlene would definitely have approved—except for my hair, of course, which looked as if it had been cut in the dark. Otherwise I looked like the kind of proper young lady a father might be proud to take to church on Sunday.

At eight I went downstairs to the lobby. I thought it best not to check out of the hotel quite yet and, in fact, told the desk clerk I'd be staying another night. Then I bought an *Oregonian* at the newsstand. There was no mention in it of my disappearance. So far, so good.

There was an armchair in the corner with a good view of the entrance and I sat there, like Wallace, behind the paper, waiting for Ryan to appear. At five minutes to nine he walked through the hotel doors. Even if I hadn't been expecting him, I would have known him right away. He was still the handsome man in the snapshot from the beach, although now he was wearing blue jeans and a faded denim jacket and dusty cowboy boots. He scanned the Benson's brass-polished lobby, pulling at a sandy mustache he had grown since he had left L.A. Finally, his eyes came to rest on me in the corner and he tentatively approached. "Meg?" he asked, not quite sure.

"Hello, Ryan." I put down the paper and rose. I didn't know whether to shake his hand or kiss him. He seemed just as uncertain, so we both stood there in uneasy silence.

"You look different than you do on TV," Ryan said at last.

"I cut my hair and dyed it."

He nodded as if that was what he had suspected, or perhaps he thought that all young girls in L.A. dyed their hair.

"Well, you're a regular young lady now, I guess."

"I'm thirteen," I said stupidly, as if he didn't know.

He nodded again. "You didn't eat breakfast, did you?" he asked.

"No."

"Good, 'cause Sheri's making waffles. C'mon." He seemed eager to escape.

We walked around the corner to where he had parked his Toyota pickup, which looked as if it had been cleaned about as long ago as his boots. He cleared the seat of tools for me and tried to dust off the torn upholstery. "Got to get this recovered," he said apologetically. Inside the cab there was a familiar odor of sawdust, but now it was difficult to match Ryan with my memories of that smell.

"Well," he said. "This was certainly a surprise, your turning up in Portland like this."

"I kind of always wanted to see the Northwest," I said. He didn't press me for anything more and seemed as ready as the desk clerk to accept the fact that I was traveling on my own.

"Well, Portland's a great place to live, an hour from the mountains, an hour from the ocean." He sounded like the magazines I had read.

"You don't miss L.A. at all?"

"Not a bit," he answered. Then realizing that L.A. included me as well, he added, "The place I mean, not you and Kelly."

I kept silent, not knowing whether to believe him or not.

"How is your brother these days?" he quickly went on. "He must be pretty big by now."

I gave Kelly a good report, careful to leave out the stuff about his problems with Darlene and his weird friends. I guess I wanted Ryan to think that we were all doing fine without him.

Maybe he sensed this, or maybe just hearing about people he had left behind made him feel uncomfortable, for he interrupted me to point out Mt. St. Helens on our left. That led to a discussion of what it was like to live in the shadow of an active volcano; it seemed a much safer topic.

Ryan drove through the city and headed up into the hills along a windy canyon road. When we had almost reached the summit, he turned off onto a narrow blacktop road that shortly became gravel. At the end of the road, built into a hillside, was a new two-story house of glass and wood. Piles of lumber and bricks and a cement mixer among the dirt and weeds of the front yard indicated that the place was still unfinished.

"Well, this is it," Ryan said as he pulled into the dirt driveway. "I still got an awful lot to do, but it's coming along."

Two Irish setters bounded out of the woods to greet us and rushed up to sniff me as I got out of the truck.

"Don't mind the dogs," Ryan assured me. "They just bark and slobber. C'mon, let me show you around," he said, suddenly at ease.

The front door opened and a tall, red-cheeked woman in blue jeans and a man's work shirt stepped out into the rubble of the front yard. Clinging to her knee was a blond little boy about three with equally red cheeks. "You got plenty of time to show her around later, Ryan," the woman said. "Right now I got waffles on the table."

"Meg," he cleared his throat, "I want you to met my wife, Sheri, and my son, Brendan."

"It's good to meet you, Meg." Sheri took my hand and shook it warmly.

I didn't have a ready reply. Even though a woman had answered the phone, I had never imagined that she might be his wife, or that they could possibly have any children.

"Aren't you going to say hello to your sister?" Sheri asked Brendan, but he seemed to be struck as dumb as I was by the discovery of our relationship. Jamming his thumb in his mouth, he hid behind Sheri's knee. I sympathized.

"We better get those waffles while they're still hot," Ryan said, leading me into the house.

The outside really didn't prepare you for how beautiful it was inside. Entering the door was like walking through the woods and suddenly discovering a spectacular view. The living room, dining room, and upstairs bedroom all opened on to a huge redwood deck that covered two sides of the house and looked out over the city, with Mt. Hood and Mt. St. Helens in the distance. I must confess, though, at that moment I wasn't concentrating too hard on the view.

We ate outside on the deck. It was obvious that Sheri had put a lot of effort into the breakfast. There were mounds of blueberry waffles, bacon, a heaping bowl of fresh fruit. She had even set the table with a centerpiece of wildflowers and a linen tablecloth on which Brendan promptly spilled maple syrup. But neither Sheri nor Ryan seemed concerned about Brendan's table manners, or those of the dogs, who raced around the deck chasing butterflies. I suppose if you lived in a house that was mostly windows and didn't have a single curtain, you wouldn't care much about things like manners.

Sheri did most of the talking. Even if she weren't Ryan's wife, I was sure Darlene wouldn't have liked her. For one thing she wasn't at all fashionable. She didn't wear makeup, her hair was just pulled together at the back of her head with a rubber band, and there were blueberry stains on her work shirt. But she had a way of drawing you into the conversation and making you feel that what you thought mattered, even if it were only about dogs or blueberries. Although I was all set to hate her, I found it hard to do. I couldn't even hate her son.

After about fifteen minutes in which Brendan did not say a single word except "booberry," he abruptly recovered his voice and then wouldn't shut up. It was easy to see why, living in that family, Ryan didn't need to say too much.

Once Brendan had gotten over his shyness, he seemed to like the idea of having me around. Before long he was tugging at my arms with his sticky hands to come and play with him. Actually, I was relieved to have an excuse to leave the table, so I followed him downstairs to see his bedroom and his toys. Except for his room, everything on the lower level was still unfinished, the walls just nailed up. It was clear that even if I wanted to move in with them, they had no place for me to stay.

After helping him build apartment houses with his "bocks," and then watching him knock them down again with relish, I was not sure I had the patience to be an older sister. "Let's make one as high as the ceiling," he said.

"I'm tired of bocks, Brendan."

"How about trucks?" he said eagerly. "Do you like to crash trucks?"

Fortunately Ryan arrived in time to rescue me and take me for the house tour he'd promised. When he first came to Portland, he explained, he had worked as a carpenter for other contractors, but he soon saw there were opportunities to go into business for himself. He had started by remodeling other people's homes and gradually progressed to building new ones. Over the last two years, in between his other work, he and Sheri had built this place themselves. Six months ago they had moved in. He was proud to show me the details of his work, explaining why he had chosen to use fir here, or redwood there, why he had decided on a round window instead of a square one. It was the most he had talked about anything that day. He spoke about carpentry with the same love that Wallace talked about acting. It made me wish he had built part of the house for me.

When our tour was over, Sheri asked if there was anything special I wanted to do. I thought for a moment. "Well, maybe we could go kite flying," I suggested. "Does Brendan have any kites?"

Ryan shook his head.

"It would be easy to go buy one, though," he said. I thought about the kite I'd brought with me. "No, it's not important," I said. "It was just a thought."

"I remember when we used to go kite flying on the beach," Ryan went on. "Do you and Kelly still do that?"

"Not anymore . . ." Not since he had left, in fact, but I didn't say it. "Do you remember the kite you gave me for my fourth birthday?"

I could see him struggling to recall it. "Sure, it was a dragon kite, wasn't it?"

"Yeah," I lied. I guess it was foolish to have expected him to remember.

"Do you still have it?" he said.

"No, it got ruined, a long time ago."

Brendan had other ideas about what to do. "I want to go to the zoo," he demanded.

"This afternoon is Meg's day," Sheri explained patiently. "I don't know if she wants to see the zoo."

"Yes, she does." He grabbed my hand. "You want to see the zoo, don't you?"

It didn't make any difference to me now, so I said the zoo was fine.

Brendan was triumphant. "I told you Meg wanted to go," he said. "She wants to see the po-er bears."

We all squeezed into the cab of the Toyota and set off. As we pulled out of the driveway, I remembered that the last time I had been to the zoo was to shoot a chewing gum commercial.

The zoo was crowded with Sunday visitors (although none were dressed as fancy as I was). Brendan clearly knew his way around the place and led me by the hand to all his favorite animals, whom he greeted like old friends. They did not appear to return his affection—not even the polar bears who stared back at us, bored and listless, from their rock ledges. I thought of the poem that Carrie had to learn for school:

I think the lion has a right,
To growl and growl and bite and bite.

Brendan wouldn't have agreed. He made me lift him so he could throw peanuts at the bears, but not even peanuts could tempt them from their shade.

"They won't eat," he complained.

"Maybe they're not hungry," Sheri said.

Brendan, however, wouldn't take no, not even from polar bears. "I want them to eat," he demanded. "Tell them to eat, Meg."

I told them, but it didn't do any good. Brendan cried.

"Let's go see the monkeys," Sheri suggested.

"Not until they eat," Brendan replied between sobs.

When Ryan picked him up and began walking away, Brendan clung to his neck and howled even louder. His tears really got to me. I took a peanut from Brendan's bag, wound up and winged it at the nearest bear, bouncing it off his snout. Lazily he reached over for it with his paw and gathered the peanut into his mouth.

I was Brendan's friend for life. He wiped his nose on his mother's jeans and led us to the monkeys.

We stayed at the zoo until Brendan's legs crumpled under him. Then Ryan lifted him to his shoulders and carried him back to the pickup where he instantly fell asleep in my lap.

That night Ryan grilled hamburgers on the deck while I helped Sheri make potato salad and corn. Brendan sat watching TV sucking his thumb.

Dinner was much quieter than breakfast. By the time we were finished, Brendan could barely keep his eyes open, but he insisted that I read him a bedtime story. He slid between the sheets and snuggled up to me in his baseball pajamas while I read *Goodnight Moon*, which I saw at once that he knew by heart. I made a few mistakes on purpose so he could correct me. He did, with great delight.

When I closed the book, Brendan put his bony little arms around my neck and gave me a sloppy wet kiss on the lips. "I like having you as a sister," he said.

"I like having you as a brother."

"You going to come and live here with us?" he asked.

"I don't know," I answered. What seemed so simple in L.A. seemed so much more complicated here. Nothing was as I had imagined.

"I want you to stay." He flopped down on his pillow as if that settled everything.

Back upstairs I found Ryan sitting alone on the deck. Dusk and rain clouds gathering over the mountains had turned the sky the color of an old bruise. I stood by the railing watching it spread and darken and waited for Ryan to begin what we had been avoiding all day.

"I figure things haven't been going so well for you in L.A.," he finally said.

"No, they haven't." In the distance there was a low rumble of thunder.

"When you called last night, out of the blue, I kind of sensed that. Then when your mom called here this morning. . . ."

"Darlene called here?" I couldn't believe it. "You didn't tell her I was here, did you?"

"She already knew, Meg. That's why she phoned."

"How? Did you call her first?"

"No, she'd hired a detective. It didn't take him long to trace you to Portland."

"Why didn't you tell me?" I was crushed. It hadn't even taken a day to find me.

"We were having such a nice time, I guess I didn't want to spoil things," he said apologetically.

"What did you tell her?"

"There wasn't much I could, just that I'd heard from you last night and that I was going to pick you up this morning. I tried to calm her down, but there's a lot between your mom and me, and she was real upset. I told her I'd try to get you to call her. Unfortunately that didn't help. As a matter of fact, she hung up on me."

"I'm not going back," I declared.

"I don't know what problems you're having with your mother," Ryan replied firmly, "but you can't solve them by running away."

"You did," I said bitterly. "You ran away and started over, and look how happy you are now."

The sun had set now behind the house and I could not see Ryan's face clearly in the deepening shadows. I knew what I'd said had hurt him, though. I had wanted to say those words for a long time, and I wasn't sorry.

"When I left you and your mom," he said at last, "I didn't know any other way. I was too young and too dumb to do anything else. There's not a day goes by that I don't wish I had been able to do it another way—a way in which I wouldn't have hurt all of you so much, a way I wouldn't have lost you and Kelly. . . ."

I said after a while, "Well, I better be going back to the hotel."

"If you don't mind sleeping on the couch, you're certainly welcome here."

"No, I think I'd rather go back."

"I'd feel a lot better if you stayed, Meg."

Maybe in the end I would have given in and stayed, if only to have had a chance to say goodbye to Brendan. But the sound of a car on the gravel cut short Ryan's attempt to persuade me. "I wonder who that could be," he said, as we hurried to the corner of the deck and peered into the darkness. I think both of us knew the answer to that question before seeing the police car. Lou had traveled with her. Only the policeman was unexpected.

"You don't have to go with her if you don't want," he said as we watched Darlene emerge from the car.

"I know," I answered.

The doorbell rang and Sheri answered it. I would like to have seen that meeting, but I could only hear Darlene's angry voice. "Is Meg here?" she demanded.

Then she saw me coming in from the deck. "Meg," she cried and ran toward me.

Ryan stepped in between us. "Wait a minute, Darlene," he said, grabbing her by the shoulders.

Furiously she tried to shake him off. "Keep your hands off me," she shouted.

In all the commotion that followed, I slipped out the front door. Perhaps I could have hidden in the woods or run to the highway and tried to hitchhike to another city, but one of Portland's famous rains was starting and I knew they'd find me sometime anyway. So I just opened the back door of the police car and got in.

RETURN

As soon as Darlene slid onto the seat next to me she started to cry. "You don't know the hell you've put us through," she wept.

Lou awkwardly patted her on the shoulder. "Hey, Meg's fine. We're all going home. Everything's going to be all right," he said with his usual optimism, but this time I don't think even he believed it.

"Oh, Meg"—Darlene tried to put her arm around me—"I'm sorry we made such a mess of this." I pulled away from her and turned my face to the window. No one said anything more until we reached the Benson. Then, pulling up to the entrance, the cop spoke for the first time. "I'd like to have a minute alone with the young lady," he said.

Lou and Darlene both looked uneasily at each other, but it was hard to say no to a policeman. I waited in the backseat, expecting a stern lecture about running away.

When we were alone, the cop turned to me and smiled. He didn't look very old, maybe just a few years out of high school. And despite his uniform he didn't look very tough. "I know it's been kind of a hard day for you," he began, "and you've got a lot of problems with your family and everything . . . and maybe this isn't the best time to ask. . . . But my kid sister's a real fan of yours. I mean she watches your show all the time, and if she knew I had you in my car and didn't get your autograph, she'd kill me. I mean it. So if you could . . ."

Unexpectedly I started to cry.

"Hey, I didn't mean to upset you," he apologized.

"That's okay," I sobbed. I felt like a fool, but the cop was very nice. He just sat there holding out a box of tissues until I finally pulled myself together. Then I autographed the back of a blank police report.

"I'm going to be a real hero," he said as he carefully folded the sheet and put it in the glove compartment.

"You take care of yourself now," he said, leading me into the hotel, "and don't let your parents push you around too much." He winked.

There were no more flights to L.A. that night, so Lou got another room at the Benson. Darlene stayed with me. "I'll say this for you, kid," Lou joked as we were going up in the elevator, "when you run away, you sure do it in style. No sleeping in doorways for you." I guess he thought if he could make me laugh, everything would be all right again.

Darlene, too, was eager to make up. "I blame myself for this," she said as we were undressing. "I knew you were unhappy, but I didn't realize how much. . . ."

I didn't answer. I didn't want to talk or think about it anymore.

"I wish you had said something to me," she went on. "We always used to be able to talk. . . . If you had just said something, maybe we would have avoided all this. . . ."

"I'm real beat," I said, slipping into my nightgown. I climbed in bed and turned my back to her.

"I just want out," I said. "That's all. Please, just leave me alone."

It wasn't easy for either of them, but Lou and Darlene both tried to keep their distance as we flew home. I sat on one side of the aisle while they sat on the other. Even so, every time I happened to glance their way, one of them was watching me, as if at any moment I might yank open the emergency exit and leap from the plane. I wondered if Darlene would let me out of her sight again.

When we landed in L.A. there was an Eyewitness News crew waiting at our exit gate. At first I thought they must be there for someone else, but when they started pointing their TV camera at us, I realized they knew about me.

"Don't say anything," Lou instructed. Gripping my shoulder, he tried to steer me around them. I wasn't very cooperative.

"Is it true you ran away from home?" a female reporter asked, thrusting the mike in my face.

"No comment," Lou answered, angrily shoving the mike away.

The reporter shoved it right back. "Why did you dye your hair, Meg?"

"This is a private matter," Lou insisted, his voice rising. "Leave her alone." He raised his arm threateningly. All the while, of course, the cameraman kept filming away, which only enraged Lou more. He tried to put his hand in front of the mini-cam to block the picture, but the cameraman expertly backed away.

In the commotion Darlene saw her chance, grabbed my arm, and yanked me to safety in the ladies' room. Hiding out in restrooms was beginning to become a habit, I thought, but we didn't need to stay there long for the television crew already had its story. I couldn't wait to see the news that night.

It was a terrific piece. Lou lost his cool so completely that the station ran his tantrum on the five, six, and eleven o'clock news. It beat the usual Monday night fare. "Is there trouble on *The Kid and the Cabbie*? Producer Lou Fleisher certainly objected to the question when Eyewitness News caught up with him today at the L.A. Airport." Kelly and I watched the story all three times.

"I can't imagine how they ever found out about you," Darlene said, shaking her head.

"Maybe it was that detective you hired," Kelly suggested.

Darlene may have believed him, but I didn't. Later that night, after she was asleep, I confronted Kelly with my suspicions.

"You're the one who called the TV station, aren't you?" I said.

"What gave me away?" He grinned.

"You've always been a lousy liar. Besides, you were the only one who knew what plane we were taking home."

"When Darlene called from Portland to say she was bringing you back, I was mad," he confessed. "I knew you wouldn't be too happy about that either, so I figured you wouldn't mind if some TV reporters showed up to greet you."

"I'm glad you did it."

"Running away was a pretty gutsy thing. Too bad you didn't get away with it."

"It wouldn't have worked out anyway. They didn't have room."

"What's our father like?" he asked softly.

"A little like you, not much of a conversationalist. I wonder if he was always that way. Do you remember?"

"I can barely even remember his face."

"He looks a lot like you, only handsomer."

Kelly threw a pillow at me.

"You know he has his own family now."

"Yeah, Darlene said."

"I liked his wife, though, and their kid is great. He's a little spoiled, but I think you'd like him anyway. He's very bright."

"He's lucky he's growing up in Portland."

"Yeah. . . . I'm quitting, you know," I blurted out.

"Is that why you ran away?"

"That and other things. . . ."

He was silent a moment.

"I guess I've been kind of tough on you, haven't I?"

"Kind of," I agreed.

"I guess I was jealous of how good you were."

"You could have been just as good if you wanted, but you quit too soon."

"I didn't quit. Nobody wanted to hire me anymore. I was all washed up, a has-been at eleven."

I had to laugh the way he said it. "You're a has-been, I'm a star. I don't know which is worse."

"When you quit, you'll have a chance to see," he said.

I don't think that anyone believed that I would really walk away from the show, least of all Kelly, but I was determined. What was the point of returning if everything was going to be the same as before?

The show was scheduled to resume production the first Monday in August. Five days before I was due back on the set, Darlene knocked on my bedroom door. She was going shopping for material for new kitchen curtains. Did I want to come along? I didn't care at all about the kitchen curtains, but I didn't have anything better to do, so I said yes.

By the time she'd found what she wanted, it was lunchtime, and Darlene suggested we eat out. "As long as we don't talk about the show," I said. "As soon as you mention Carrie, I'm gone."

Darlene promised.

It was a very quiet lunch until Darlene asked for a second cup of coffee. Then, as if she had been preparing for this awhile, she said, "You know, I've been doing a lot of thinking since we came home."

"You promised," I warned.

"This isn't about the show," she said. "It's about me."

I nodded for her to continue.

"When I was your age I was pretty difficult to get along with. Your grandma and I were at each other all the time. I swore that when I grew up and had kids I wouldn't make the same mistakes. . . . Well, I didn't make the same mistakes as Grandma, but I made lots of others. . . .

"I've been thinking that maybe I shouldn't have pushed you and Kelly into show business so young . . . but it was what I wanted when I was your age and I thought it was what you wanted, too. You have so much talent, Meg. I thought it would make you happy. . . ."

"I'm not you," I said.

"We are different," she admitted. "I realize now that I can't make your decisions for you." She looked at me intently. "Whatever you decide, though, I hope it's what you really want."

"It will be," I said. But suddenly I was not so sure.

Telling Rhonda and Lou I was quitting was one thing. Telling Wallace was another. That was one conversation I wasn't looking forward to. That very night he called.

"Tell him I'm not here," I told Darlene.

"Too late. I already said you're home."

"Some correspondent you turned out to be," he said when I lifted the receiver.

"I'm sorry," I apologized. "I started a letter to you, but I never finished it."

"I guess you were otherwise occupied."

"Sort of . . ." I didn't know how much he knew.

"My dear, even in Williamstown, Massachusetts, it's impossible to escape the news from Hollywood. A friend of mine taped Lou's little scene at the airport for me, so I had a chance to see it today when I got home. I thought he gave a marvelous performance."

"Me, too," I laughed.

"Look, I want you to come sailing with me tomorrow."

"I. . . I don't think I can," I tried begging off.

"Of course you can," he insisted. "I'll pick you up at ten o'clock. Be ready." He hung up.

The next morning, five minutes early, Wallace appeared in our doorway wearing a captain's hat. He held his ever-present cigar to the side to give Darlene a buss on the cheek, scattering ashes in the entrance hall. Then he hurried me out the door.

"So," he said, as we sped down the street in his old MG, "some kind of runaway you turned out to be. You didn't even last three days on the lam."

It sounded funny the way he said it.

"You know when I was sixteen, I ran away, too," he said. "Set out for New York City to make my fortune, only I got lost on the way and ended up in the Catskills instead. Changed my life." I was glad he seemed ready to do all the talking. On the way to his Malibu home he recounted the whole crazy story of how he had left his family and their cramped apartment above his father's tailor shop in Nanticoke, Pennsylvania, and ended up a busboy in the Catskills. Watching the great stand-up comics perform night after night, he decided he wanted to become a comedian himself. Only World War II intervened and he went off to England to fight.

By the time we had reached his beachfront home, the Allies had won the war, although Wallace himself had not fired a single shot; instead he had spent his entire military career in London keeping track of food supplies. "Once a busboy, always a busboy," he quipped. On his return to America, he finally arrived in New York City. He knew then that although he could tell a good joke, he was not so good at inventing them. So he decided to become an actor instead of a comedian.

Wallace lived in a small, old-fashioned, white clapboard house that looked out of place among the taller, more modern glass and concrete buildings that surrounded it. His wife was gone for the afternoon, but she had left us a picnic cooler filled with drinks and sandwiches. We carried it down the rickety white steps to where Wallace had beached his fourteen-foot blue-and-white fiberglass sailboat.

"Tell me about getting started in New York," I asked.

"Later," he said. "I can talk, smoke, and drive a car at the same time, but I haven't learned yet to talk, smoke, and launch my sail-boat."

For Wallace sailing was serious business. Although he did not appear to be too athletic, he was a surprisingly good sailor. I helped him a little, but he was clearly used to doing everything himself. He shifted sails with the changing wind, steered the boat as easily as his MG. The day was clear and sunny and there was a brisk ocean breeze; it was not long before his house looked as small as a dollhouse in the distance.

When we had traveled far enough from shore to satisfy Wallace, he adjusted the sails and let the boat drift. Then he opened the cooler and passed me a chicken sandwich.

"Now tell me about New York," I urged.

"No, I've already talked too much about myself. It's time to talk about you."

"You're much more interesting," I protested.

"I'm the captain of the ship. I'll decide that," he asserted. "Now what's this I hear about you leaving the show?"

"Did Lou tell you to talk to me?" I asked.

"Young lady," he answered sternly, "there are not many people I invite out on my boat, and certainly none because Lou Fleisher asked me. If you think I brought you out here to try to convince you to stay on that silly show, we might as well go back now."

He grabbed the tiller and turned the boat toward shore.

"You don't care if I leave then?"

"Of course I care. For my own selfish reasons I'll miss you, but I would never for a moment presume to stop you if you thought it was time to move on."

"Then if I quit and the show fails, you won't hate me?"

"My dear," he started to laugh. "Oh, Meg. . ." The sailboat rocked with his laughter. "Whoever gave you the idea that if the show fails it will be your fault? *I*," he gestured theatrically with his cigar, "am the star of this show, not you. If the show fails, it will be *my* fault."

I suddenly started to giggle, too. It was silly to think that either of us could single-handedly save Lou's show. "Now, is that settled?" he asked. "Can we continue with this sail?" He steered the boat back out to sea.

"The truth is," he went on, "however much either of us would like to think we're irreplaceable, we're not. No actor ever is. I know Lou doesn't want to lose you, but I also know he has at least three other girls waiting in the wings if you don't return. The show always goes on."

It was the first time I'd thought of Lou actually replacing me, and I didn't like the idea of someone else playing Carrie. "What do you think I should do?" I asked.

"I can't tell you that."

"Why not? Everybody else is. Why don't you?"

"Because it doesn't matter what I think. Besides, I could only say what I might do if I were in your place. But I'm not you and I wouldn't have to live with the consequences, so my advice would be worthless."

I knew that he was right. Still, I wanted him to tell me the best choice. "Why did you even invite me here, anyway?" I said resentfully.

"When I heard you might be leaving, I realized that there were some things I've been meaning to say to you, and I wanted to make sure I got a chance to say them." He paused, adjusting a sail.

"Have you ever heard of the Hollywood blacklist?"

"No, is it something I should know about?"

"Unfortunately, it is." He sounded sad. "There was a period during the late forties and fifties when many people in the movie industry were denied work because of their political beliefs. I was one of them."

"You were on a blacklist?"

He nodded, took a long pull of his cigar. "It's a very long story, and maybe another time I'll tell it all to you, but the end result is that for ten years I was unable to get work. Not on stage, in television, or the movies. Nobody would hire me."

"That's awful," I said. "What did you do all that time?"

"Oh, I survived. I was young, unmarried then. That made it easier. I painted houses for a while, sold insurance, eventually managed a restaurant. But the point is, and this is really why I wanted to tell you this story, I discovered something very important about myself during those ten years. I discovered I *had* to act, that for me not being able to act was like losing my eyesight or my powers of speech. I wasn't really alive."

He paused, stared at the water for a moment, then looked back at me. "In that respect I think you and I are very much alike. I don't know if you realize how important acting is to you yet, but I think it is as essential a part of you as it is me. You also happen to have been blessed with a rare ability to make people laugh or cry by your performance. I don't think you have any idea how rare a gift it is, and how few actors and actresses really have it, but you do. . . ."

"I don't know," I said. "Sometimes I wish I had never started in show business."

"I can understand that," he answered. "The ten years I couldn't work I often felt that way. If I hadn't known the joy of acting, I thought, then I would never have missed it so much. I guess right now acting feels the same way to you, like a curse rather than a gift. But the one piece of advice I will give you is this: whatever you decide about the show, don't turn your back on your talent just because of the way other people have tried to use it."

He puffed on his cigar, but it had gone out. "Someday I'm going to give up this dirty habit," he said and tossed the butt into the ocean. I watched it float in the wake of the boat and finally sink. I was not sure that I understood everything that he had said to me. There was a lot I'd never thought about before, but I didn't feel like trying to make sense of it all at that moment.

"Okay, enough of talking about me," I said. "If you're the real

star of the show, then you have to tell me how you got to be one."
So he did. For the rest of the afternoon he entertained me with
stories of his past, and later that night when he drove me home, I
realized that we had not said another word about *The Kid and the
Cabbie*. But whether or not I returned to the show suddenly didn't
seem that important anymore.

From "Growing Up a Star," the cover story of *TV Guide:*

Thirty-two-year-old Darlene Muldaur looks more like a glamorous actress than the stage mother she has been for the last seven years. Her views on show biz mothers are as fresh as her looks. "People say I don't want my child in the business. Don't believe it. I think every parent would like to have their kid be a star. Let's be realistic. All the pampering and glamour and excitement. How can a child not love it?

"Besides I think show business is good for children. The more kids have to do, the less trouble they get into. Show business gives them a sense of discipline. It gives them something more to be excited about than playing video games.

"Working in TV keeps our kids off the street and gives them an experience that no school and no amount of money can buy, but everyone thinks of stage mothers as bad. They see us as wicked witches standing in the wings forcing our children to go on. I don't think that describes me at all. Meg and Kelly have always made up their own minds about their careers. I advise them, but they make the final decisions. If Meg wanted to quit tomorrow, she could. Kelly basically has."

WE ALL TAKE
A MEETING

Maybe leaving the show would have gotten back at Lou and Darlene for dragging me home; still, after my sail with Wallace, I realized that it would have hurt me more. Besides I wanted to continue working with Wallace. I knew how much I could still learn from him.

Right after breakfast on Saturday morning I phoned Rhonda. She recognized my voice immediately. "I wondered if you were ever going to call," she said.

I got right to the point. "I've made up my mind what I want to do," I told her.

"You're going back, I hope."

"I think we need to have a meeting about this," I said. "You, me, Darlene, Lou." Before I went back, I wanted a few changes.

"You're not even going to tell your own agent what you've decided?" she said.

"At the meeting."

"Have you told your mother?"

"Rhonda, you're the very first person I called."

She was not impressed. "Let me speak to Darlene," she demanded.

I put Darlene on the phone, and they quickly made plans for that afternoon.

"I'm glad you've made up your mind," Darlene said after she hung up. "I think you should know I've made a decision, too."

"What about?" I said in surprise.

"Well..." She suddenly seemed a little embarrassed. "Rhonda is expanding her office and she's asked me to come to work for her. And I've said yes."

"Hey, that's great!"

She looked at me uncertainly. "You really think so? I'm a little nervous about it. I've never had a job like this before."

I really was happy for her.

"Oh, you'll be fine," I said encouragingly. "After all the auditions you've taken Kelly and me to, you probably know as much about the business as Rhonda."

"That's what she said, too." She seemed pleased.

Before we left for Rhonda's I took Kelly aside and told him what I was going to do. He reacted as if that's what he had expected all along.

"You're not angry at me for changing my mind, are you?" I asked.

He shook his head. "You'd be miserable going to junior high school all year. You're not cut out to be just a regular kid."

"But you don't hate me for it, do you?"

"No more than usual." He grinned. "I mean if you can put up living with a has-been, then I suppose I can put up living with a star."

At one that afternoon, Darlene, Lou, Rhonda, and I all gathered at Rhonda's Sunset Boulevard office. This year she had painted the walls a salmon pink. Her nails were apricot, but today her eyelids were plain. I wasn't sure if it was a new style or if she was a little nervous about our meeting.

She gave me a warm hug, then got right down to business. "This is your scene, dear. You play it."

The three of them sat back on Rhonda's blue chairs, that now clashed with the walls, and waited for me to begin. "I'm willing to return," I said, "but *only* on certain conditions." I paused for dramatic effect. It had been a long time since I had enjoyed a part so much.

Rhonda shifted impatiently in her chair.

"I'm listening," Lou replied.

"First, no more parties," I declared.

"Fine," Lou immediately agreed.

"Second, no more interviews with the press. . . ."

"I don't know if I can do that, Meg," he protested. "I don't know if the network will let me."

"Wallace only does a few interviews a year," I argued. "I'll do as many as he does."

"The network's not going to like it," he said.

I shrugged. I was pretty sure he could convince them if he wanted. "And no more visits to hospitals," I added.

"The hospitals I can guarantee," he said. "The interviews I'll have to see about. But I promise I'll cut them down. Promise."

"Okay." I was willing to compromise a little. "Next, I don't want Carrie to turn into an air-brained, boy-crazed teenager."

Lou winced. "Do you really think I'd do that to Carrie?" he defended himself. "I know we've had our differences, Meg, but give me a break. Believe me, I'll never turn Carrie into an airhead."

"I just wanted to be sure."

"You can count on it. Now what else?"

I turned to Darlene. "I'm not sure about this, but I've been thinking that I might like to try a private school next year. . . ."

"I was going to suggest the same thing," Darlene immediately approved. "A small private school might be much easier."

"Anything else?" Lou asked.

"Well, there is one more thing. . . ." I reached into the back pocket of my jeans and pulled out the crumpled business card of the cabbie who drove me to the airport. "There's a writer I know I want you to give a chance to. I think he has a real feeling for the show."

Lou examined the now barely legible card with suspicion. "C'mon, Meg," he said, "it's one thing to insist on limiting interviews, it's something else to ask to hire the writers, too."

"I think he might be very good." I held my ground.

Lou shook his head. "I want you back, kid, but you drive a hard bargain. . . ."

"How can you know if he's any good or not unless you talk to him?" I asked.

"All right," he reluctantly gave in, "if you really want me to, I'll talk to this guy. I can't guarantee anything, but I'll listen to his ideas. If they're any good, he gets a shot. Fair enough?"

"Fair enough," I agreed.

"Okay, what else?"

There really wasn't anything else. The rest I had to do myself. "That's it." I grinned.

"That's all?" He beamed.

"Not so fast," Rhonda interrupted. "I think we ought to talk about money, too. It just happens that Meg has never signed that new contract we worked out in June."

"I wondered when you were going to bring that up." Lou sighed. "All right, we'll talk dollars, but you and me, kid,"—he turned to me—"we're all square now, right?"

"Right."

"Welcome back then." He got up and hugged me. To my surprise, I hugged him back.

"I had a feeling things might work out," he said, "so I brought a little present in case they did." He stepped into the hall and a moment later reappeared wheeling a silver Fuji ten-speed. "It's kind of a belated birthday gift," he said.

"It's beautiful, Lou," I exclaimed.

"It should be," he said. "The guy at the bike shop told me it's the Mercedes of bicycles."

Then I noticed a script fastened to the rear of the bike with a red ribbon. I untied the ribbon and looked at the cover page. The title was "Runaway" and Lou had written it himself.

"I wrote this specially for you," he said. "It's a two-parter."

"What's it about?" I asked.

"Well, in the first part Tony throws a surprise birthday party for Carrie even though she's told him she doesn't want one. Tony's so proud of her, though, that he wants to show her off and invites all his friends and a lot of kids Carrie can't stand. She gets so mad at him that she runs away."

"I don't know where you ever got an idea like that," I said.

He winked.

"What happens in the second part?" I asked.

"What else? Tony tracks her down and brings her back. Carrie learns she can't run away every time she has a problem, and Tony learns he has to listen more. . . ."

"Then they go back to insulting each other again."

"Of course."

If Lou and I could make up, I thought, maybe there was hope for Carrie and Tony, too, and their future together on TV. "I'll read the script tonight," I said.

"I hope you like it."

"If I don't, I'll tell you," I promised. "I happen to know a few things about running away."